THE LINTHEAD MURDERS

Don Bailey

Mill Hill Press

ISBN-10:0692344837
ISBN-13:978-0692344835

PROLOGUE

Because its specific gravity was very close to that of the water, the body initially floated just below the surface. Gradually however, as air in the lungs was replaced by water, it sank five or six feet to rest on the muddy bottom of the pond. At that depth there was essentially no current and the body rested without moving for the better part of a day. But the water was very warm, and the millions, or billions, of bacteria in the stomach, intestines and chest cavity were not slow to begin busily producing methane, hydrogen sulfide, and carbon dioxide. As these gases formed, the specific gravity of the body decreased and, inch by sluggish inch, it rose to the surface of the pond. Here there was a small but significant current, and the body floated, at not much more than glacial speed, unnoticed through the night.

DAY ONE

Forrest Hames stopped outside the entrance to the weave room. Even though it was a hot Monday morning in July, Forrest was wearing his customary three piece suit. He reached into the pocket of his vest and consulted his watch. It was seven thirty and he, like most of the people in the village, had been up since five thirty. He looked around at his plant and, though the textile plant itself and the sloping hillside meant he could see almost none of it, he raised his eyes to the roadway, beyond and about which, his village lay. It was indeed his village. He had seen to the building of the plant, the school, the company store, the dwelling houses and every other thing required to make the village of Boiling Springs self-contained. And while it was true that Boiling Springs Mills owned the plant and village, Hames owned the majority share of Boiling Springs Mills.

Forrest had every reason to feel satisfied with himself. He was still healthy and vigorous here in his sixty-third year. He had survived the panic of 1907. And he found himself possessed of the largest gingham mill in the Southeast. But he would not allow himself too much pride, for he was a religious man. Not a religious man of the snake handling, speaking in tongues, rolling in the aisles variety found at the tent revivals that passed through occasionally, but a religious man of the sort who believed the deadly sins were indeed deadly. If asked, he would have said he believed the Bible was the literal word of God—

but he would have found some way to get around that admonition to sell all you have and give to the poor.

Hames stepped through the weave room door and was instantly submerged in the roar of the looms and wrapped in the almost sweet smell of cotton. At each loom a shuttle was literally being thrown by picker arms back and forth through tents of thread, tents that were constantly formed and reformed by the harnesses raising and lowering threads coming off the top and bottom warps, thereby creating patterns in the cloth being woven. Both the heads of the picker arms and the tips of the shuttle itself were covered with iron. Thus every second at every loom there was a report as shuttle met picker head, a report that was very like a hammer striking a nail. And the air was filled with a thin, almost invisible cloud of cotton lint. The cotton lint was scraped off threads as they were pulled and pushed by the looms. When people wanted to denigrate the operatives of textile plants—those who had chosen, or been forced, to leave the farm and take up what was called "public work"—they did so by calling them "lintheads." Of course by day's end it was not merely the head of the worker that was covered with lint, it was the entire body—outside and, to some degree, inside as well.

Forrest Hames did not know he practiced management by walking around, but that was indeed what he did—when he was not occupied with buying land or planning an addition to the plant, or village. This morning he walked through the weave room eyeing the looms and the weavers who watched over them. He stopped at the head of one of the "alleys"—double rows of looms facing each other—to watch a bobbin boy dumping bobbins from the collection cans attached to the side of each loom into a large wheeled wooden box. These bobbins had been ejected from the shuttles as they had become empty. They would be taken to the spinning room on the floor above to be refilled. Most of the weavers were simply walking their part of the alley, that section of ten or twelve looms assigned to them. Occasionally a weaver would be bent over one of their looms tying in a

Jim Henry watched the doctor hurry across the town square. "Looks like Callie's knees are hurtin' him again." He then turned to the undertaker. "Anything you can tell me, Amos? You've seen yore share of dead people."

Amos cleared his throat. "I ain't seen that many shot though—this 'un and one more. T'other one was shot with a thirty eight, right in the eye. But I think Snag must've been standin' by the river and the shot knocked him in. If he was killed somewhere else, why not leave him there? Why'd you want to carry 'im and dump 'im in the river?"

Jim Henry nodded. "That seems right. But is they any place where the bank drops off away from the river? How could he have been standin' on the bank and him who shot 'im standin' lower down?"

"I don't rightly know, Jim Henry."

The constable looked at the bales of cotton stacked to the rafters in the warehouse. Then he looked at the floor, "Well Amos, it's yore place to take care of Snag, and my place to find who killed him. Guess I'll see the sheriff's notified, and then take a walk along the river bank."

Jim Henry left the warehouse, crossed the southeast corner of the square, and went into the mill office. There he used the only phone in town to inform the sheriff's office of the murder.

Leaving the mill office the constable decided he should head home and eat before searching along the river bank. He crossed the square, and as he was taking Main Street north toward the avenue on which he lived, Jim Henry noticed Rat Tail Summie coming his way, no doubt also headed home to eat his lunch—what everyone in the village called dinner. Rat Tail was a short, somewhat chubby man in his late thirties. He was a clerk in the men's clothing section of the company store, and—perhaps for that reason—he was always careful of his dress. His name was actually Ralph Yale Summie, but at some point this had morphed into Rat Tail, the name by which he was known to everyone in the village. Only his wife called him Ralph.

Jim Henry waited for Rat Tail to catch up with him, and they walked together. Rat Tail had a bruised and swollen cheek and Jim Henry asked what had happened.

"Well Jim Henry, I don't want to be short with you," Rat Tail said, "but it was my wife, my rolling pin, and it's my business." Rat Tail then chuckled.

Jim Henry felt he was also obliged to chuckle, and so he did. But he thought Rat Tail may well have told more truth than he really wanted known. Rat Tail's wife, Eloise, was a tall, thin, bony woman—a woman notoriously harsh and bossy. She had few friends, and the verbal and physical brawls she had with Rat Tail were legendary in the village. There was an embarrassed silence as the men walked along, and Jim Henry was relieved when he said goodbye to Rat Tail and turned into his street.

* * *

At thirty six, Joann Tate was five years younger than Jim Henry. She was also six inches shorter and four years more educated. She seldom wore makeup, and when she did, it was never more than a light lipstick. Jim Henry thought she was a bit thin, and as pretty as any woman he'd ever seen, perhaps prettier. She, privately, thought her breasts too small and her face too long.

As Jim Henry entered the kitchen, Joann smiled and said, "You're late, Law Man. Have you caught who killed Snag?"

Jim Henry pulled out a chair from the kitchen table, sat, and replied, "Not yet, but I think it might be Rat Tail's wife. Rat Tail sure looks like she took a try at doin' away with him sometime recent. If you ask me, that woman's just plain mean."

Joann sighed, "Well, she sure puts on airs. She comes from dirt poor mountain folk just like the rest of us. But since Rat Tail doesn't work in the mill she thinks she's too good for most all the village." She shook her head. "That woman! Poor Rat Tail will never have enough to satisfy her."

"Exactly how do you mean 'enough to satisfy her?'" asked Jim Henry with a grin.

Joann put a plate of pinto beans, turnip greens and cornbread in front of Jim Henry and swatted him on the head with a dish towel.

"If you're thinking what I think you're thinking, forget it. It's too hot for any of that."

Joann was eager to discuss what she might write about the murder. She took great pride in her column in the small county newspaper, reporting events in the village. Of course it was only rarely that the events reported rose above social gatherings and church meetings. The report of a teacher being hired, or a small business opening—or changing hands—was big news indeed. An event such as a murder in the village had never been reported!

"Now seriously Jim Henry, what can I say about Snag's killing? He was found on the dam; he was shot in the chest. What else?"

"That's all I know. I'm just gettin' started here. No suspects, no nothin'."

After a moment Joann said, "I guess I can describe how his body was recovered from the dam. And what did Dr. Callahan have to say?"

"He pretty much said Snag was shot."

"Oh come on! Surely there's something else."

Because his full mouth prohibited any reply, Jim Henry merely shook his head.

* * *

One block west of, and parallel to Main, was the railroad. Then one more half block west, and parallel to the railroad, was Railroad Street. Immediately west of Railroad Street was the river. In fact, those living in houses on the west side of Railroad Street could very nearly fish from their back windows. At the north end of Railroad Street was a small park with a bandstand. North of the bandstand there were no houses along the railroad for about a quarter mile. Then the black section of the village began, running along both sides of the railroad. This part of the village was called, by black and white alike, simply "The Line". Houses along The Line were farther from the river, which by this time ran not due north, but northwest. About a half mile further upriver from The Line, Corn Mill Creek ran into the river from the east. The east side of the river from the dam to the creek was used by the folk living in the village. Jim Henry was sure Snag had gone into the river somewhere along that stretch. North of the creek, and all along the west bank of the river, there was nothing but poison ivy, briars, weeds, snakes, scrub pine, and an occasional hardwood; no one used those areas.

Jim Henry passed the bandstand and walked to the river's edge. South of the spot where he stood, the river bank was clear of brush all the way to the dam, with only an occasional tree. The village was only eight years old and the river bank had been cleared when the houses and the park were built. Since then the park had been continually maintained, as had the back yards of most of the houses along the bank. But to the north of the little park there was simply a path running along the east edge of the river through underbrush and trees. This had to be the area where Snag was killed. Jim Henry walked upstream and noticed that, as he had thought, the land either rose or remained level as one moved away from the river bank. He could see no place where Snag could have been standing on the river bank with his assailant standing below him.

Soon the sound of children laughing and water splashing caught Jim Henry's attention. He knew this would be children who lived on The Line. The white children all swam in what was called the village pool, though it was just a deep spot in a creek. Puzzle Creek ran into the river on the southeast side of the village, and up that creek, about fifty yards before it emptied into the river, a makeshift dam created a small pond some twenty feet long, fifteen feet across, and three to four feet deep.

Walking along the river bank, the constable soon saw seven young, naked, black boys playing in the water. A rope had been tied to a tree limb jutting out above the river. On this rope the boys were swinging over the river and letting go to splash into the water, which at this point was some five or six feet deep. When the boys saw Jim Henry they immediately fell silent. The four on the shore stood rigid, as did two others who were near the bank. Only the boy who was so far out in the river that he could not touch the stream bottom kept moving, treading water and looking at Jim Henry.

The constable smiled. "Hello boys. It's a good day for swimming. You boys being careful are you?"

Almost in unison the boys said, "Yes sir, Mr. Jim Henry."

To the boy treading water in the middle of the stream Jim Henry said, "Come on in son, I wanna talk to you boys."

The boy continued to tread water, not moving toward shore.

"Come on now boys. You all come on up here on the bank. You ain't done nothin' wrong. I just need yer help."

Slowly and in complete silence the boys assembled on the river bank, all eyes trained on the constable.

"Okay," began Jim Henry, "you boys heard about Mr. Snag ain't you?"

At first it seemed no one would speak. Finally one boy, who appeared to be the youngest of the group, said, "Yes sir, Mr. Jim Henry. He got kilt."

"That's right, and you know I'm the constable. So I have to catch the one who killed him. Now I bet you boys are around down here on the river and in these woods right much, ain't you?"

This time three of the boys volunteered, "Yes sir, Mr. Jim Henry."

"Well what I'd like to know is if you heard or saw anything yesterday or Saturday that I ought to know about. Did you see Mr. Snag down here? Did you hear any fights down this way? Hear any arguments?"

This time the boys looked at Jim Henry with wide eyes but no one spoke.

"Boys, you know you ought to tell me anything you heard or saw, don't you?"

This question got a quick and all but unanimous "Yes sir, Mr. Jim Henry."

Jim Henry waited for someone to say something more. No one did, and he gave up. "Okay boys, y'all take care in that river now."

It was about a half mile further north to the mouth of the creek. Jim Henry expected there was no area along there where the ground fell away from the river bank. But he decided to complete his inspection and he began walking north. As soon as he was out of their sight, he heard the boys yelling and laughing again.

The constable walked to the mouth of Corn Mill Creek and stood for quite a few minutes wondering what he should do next. Finally he decided he would go over to the trade lot at Sunshine, just two miles or so east of the village. By now everyone would certainly be gossiping about Snag. And the gossip should be thickest and juiciest at Sunshine, where horse traders, loafers, gamblers and general ne'er-do-wells gathered. Walking south, back toward the village, Jim Henry soon heard the young black boys once again. Just at the time he heard the boys, he noticed something he had not seen on his walk up to the creek. On the south edge of a path leading from the river to The Line, the path along which the young boys had doubtless come, there was a piece of green checked oilcloth. He had not seen it earlier because the cloth was almost hidden under a growth of ferns. Oilcloth was a heavy cotton cloth with a linseed oil coating. It was used most often as a tablecloth, for it was almost waterproof and spills were easily wiped off. Jim Henry picked up the cloth. It was a piece about four feet long and perhaps two feet wide. It looked almost new. Why, he wondered, had the cloth been thrown away? After a moment he shrugged, rolled up the oilcloth, and took the path toward The Line.

When he reached the black quarter of the village Jim Henry began walking south along the railroad track. As he met The Line's residents he greeted them by name and they courteously responded with, "How do constable," "Mr. Jim Henry," or simply "Cap'n." At the south end of The Line was a little café which, along with the AME church, at the north end, formed the social center for the black citizens of Boiling Springs. Jim Henry stepped to the door of the café and stopped for his eyes to adjust to the dim interior. Soon he was able to make out that only two men were in the café, June Wallace and Elvy Foster. June, a light skinned black man of medium build was about fifty years of age. He ran the café independently, although he rented the building itself. The café building—like every buildings in the village—was owned by Boiling Springs Mills. Elvy Foster was thin and in his early sixties. His skin was so black it seemed almost purple in certain light. Elvy usually worked as fireman on the little train that ran some three or so miles to a junction with the Seaboard. He had severely sprained his ankle a few days earlier when he missed his footing jumping from the tender.

"Morning June, Elvy, you all seem to be taking it easy."

"Ain't no other way I can take it Cap'n," said Elvy. "I got to set 'round 'til this ankle of mine fix itself."

June smiled and said, "Ain't nobody spending they money right now, so I'm settin' and gittin' pore."

"Well, you could help me if you'd tell me who shot ole Snag."

"Ain't nobody on The Line, that's for sure," said June. "But, if you 'scuse me Cap'n, ain't nobody gonna be sorry to see Mr. Snag go. He had a mean streak."

Noise from the train making its afternoon freight run caused the men to stop their conversation and watch as the engine puffed by with three cars in tow. When quiet returned Jim Henry said, "You're right June, Snag was no shinin' example for young folks to follow; have to admit that. But seriously now, he must have been shot somewhere on the river not far from The Line. Did you boys hear anything Saturday night, yesterday early, maybe Friday night?"

Both men merely looked at the constable. Finally Elvy said, "I don't know if anybody hear anything or not. But this here's white folks business and black folks gonna try they best to stay out of it."

"Elvy, you can't withhold evidence on me now. That can get you locked up right quick."

"I ain't withholdin' no evidence, Mr. Jim Henry. I'm just sayin' people on The Line gonna be quieter than usual when you come askin' about any white man getting kilt." Elvy looked at the floor and shook his head. Then he looked up at the constable and said, "You know that Cap'n."

"Yeah, I know, I know. And I ain't really threatenin' to jail nobody. But I can't have folks shootin' one another. And you boys are two of the leaders on The Line. You're good Christians I know. You can't think it's right that even ole Snag got shot, and if you can help me out, you ought to."

After a long pause in which the two men sat mute and looked at him, Jim Henry said, "Well, if you learn anything about this business it's yore place to let me know. And I hope you will. You know me. I've always tried to be fair with ever body, includin' all you folks on The Line. Anything any of you all tell me won't go no further."

The constable turned to go and then turned back. "June, you got any use for this piece of oilcloth? Found it down on the river. It's too little for a tablecloth."

"Sure, I can find a use for it," June replied.

Elvy laughed. "I know what that oilcloth been used for. Somebody been sowin' human seed down yonder, and this cloth keepin' some young lady's butt off the ground."

Jim Henry left and walked south along the track for about a quarter mile. He then turned east and made his way to the livery stable near the north east corner of the village—that is, the north east corner of the white portion of the village. At the stable, the operator, Scott Blanton, was mending harness while a teen age black boy was mucking out stalls.

"Morning Scott, I need a horse. I'm about to ride over to Sunshine."

"What's happenin' over there? Somebody sellin' moonshine?"

"Well, I expect so. If not, it'll probably be the first time. But right now I'm more interested in who killed Snag. I'm goin' huntin' for gossip. You heard anything?"

"Not really." Scott looked around for the stable boy, lowered his voice and said, "Seems like our coloreds over on The Line had no love for Snag though. Reckon one of them could've killed him?"

"No reason to think so, and I sure hope not. I hate to think what a ruckus they'd be if that was so."

"Yeah. Then too, I guess not all that many white folks had any use for Snag."

"He was a rough 'un."

"But I hear he was a good smash hand."

"That's what they say. You know when one of them shuttles busts out on a loom it'll take out a couple hundred or more threads. Hard to understand how a man as rough as Snag could do that fine work, tyin' in all them broke ends."

* * *

Heading for Sunshine, the constable took the road heading east from the town square. The road crossed Puzzle Creek about a hundred yards from the square. Then for a half mile or so village houses lined the south side of the road. Nothing but woodland bordered the road for the next quarter mile. Then the forest opened up into sprawling farmland outside the village, that is to say outside the Boiling Springs Mills property.

It was near four o'clock when Jim Henry tied his horse in front of the small café at the trade lot. There were few men around; and this was not the place one expected to find women.

The Henson brothers sat under a tree that was near a pen containing four cows and a mule. The constable walked over, "You boys sellin' cows, or mules?"

"Howdy, Jim Henry. I reckon we're sellin' nothin' today. How about you buy a cow? We'd make the law a real good price," said the older of the two.

"I don't believe I need a cow. Where's yer daddy? Is he over in Tennessee buyin' more mules?"

"Might not be in Tennessee right yet; he left yesterday. He

plans on bringin' 'round forty mules back this time, if he can git 'em cheap enough."

"Well, I hope he has a good trip. But I'm here lookin' to git some information about Snag. You boys know anything I ought to know?"

The younger boy giggled and said, "I expect we know what ever body knows. Snag beat ole Rafer Jones so bad last week he near killed him."

"Now that's right interestin'. How come I didn't know that? Where'd it happen?"

The older boy slapped his brother on the head, turned to Jim Henry and said, "I reckon we ought not be tellin' this. But since simple shit here's let the cat out, Saturday night a week ago Rafer had some words with Snag at that beer joint just over the state line. Snag wound up and smacked Rafer 'cross the mouth. Well then, Rafer went out to his horse where he had a pistol. He come back in, stuck that pistol in Snag's face and pulled the trigger."

"You don't say!"

"It's the God's truth, and wouldn't you know that thing didn't fire? Well, with that Snag caught Rafer up side his head with a bottle. If people hadn't pulled Snag off him, it'd be Rafer what's dead."

Jim Henry shook his head, "Well I'll be, what got this all started in the first place? What was Rafer and Snag havin' words about?"

The two brothers looked at each other. Then the younger said, "Don't know for sure. But I think it was about some woman."

"Must've been about Snag screwin' some woman. You reckon that was it, or what?"

"Can't say, Jim Henry. Not even sure that's what started it. But folks at the café seem to think they was a woman at the cause of it."

"I appreciate you boys letting me know about this. You reckon Rafer tried Snag one more time, and this time they wasn't no misfire?"

"Could've been; I bet it was hard for Rafer to take that beatin' and just tuck his tail 'tween his legs."

The constable left the two boys and walked over to the café. As he entered, someone called out, “Ever body hide yore licker.”

“Ha ha; yeah that’s funny,” said Jim Henry. “Don’t think I don’t know they’s a lot of shine passes through this hell hole.”

Joe Kenny, the owner of the café and trade lot, sat with two older men at one of the café’s three tables. One of the men asked, “Who killed ole Snag?”

“If I knew that I wouldn’t be here disturbin’ you fine gentlemen this afternoon. What can you all tell me about Snag’s killin’?”

The three men just sat quietly. One shook his head and said, “Snag run with a rough crowd. You oughta ask some of them.”

“I plan to, but they’s some people work for a livin’. Snag’s crowd’s all at work in the plant. Come on now, what’s this I hear about Snag and Rafer?”

“I don’t know nothin’ about that,” one of the men replied. “But I know Rafer ain’t been around in a while. Somebody did say he was laid up at home and couldn’t work.”

Jim Henry sighed. “But I hear they’s been talk in this very café that Rafer and Snag had a quarrel about some woman, and that quarrel got real nasty.”

“Well lotsa folks talk in this café,” said the owner. “Don’t mean the three of us know anything.”

Jim Henry was suddenly sick of dancing around. Before his better judgment could kick in he said, “Bull shit! You fellers do nothin’ but set around here and collect gossip—and spread it too. Just wait ‘til the next time somebody crosses the line in here, or at that trade lot. I’ll come down on ever body in sight like a load of brick. Now who is the woman that got Snag and Rafer crosswise?”

No one volunteered a comment and Jim Henry stormed out.

Riding back to the village the constable calmed down and decided his visit had not been completely useless. It could very well be that Rafer Jones had killed Snag. He’d have to visit Rafer and see what he could learn. But he thought he’d leave that visit until the next day. The more he found out before talking with Rafer, the more he was likely to get from him. Jim Henry decided he would sit around a while and then visit Snag's house later on to see who sat with the corpse. Probably it would be some of Snag's buddies and some of them would probably be well lubricated with moonshine. Maybe their tongues would be loosened up some.

* * *

At about seven thirty Jim Henry walked over to the south east corner of the village, to the little three room house in which Snag Wiley had originally lived with his family, in which he later lived alone, and in which his coffin now rested on two sawhorses.

The front room of the little house was filled to capacity with a dozen straight back chairs and the coffin. Amos had chosen to close the coffin and there was a chemical smell the constable couldn't identify. Jim Henry thought neighbors must have brought in the chairs, for Snag would surely not have owned more than three or four. Five chairs were occupied by men in their mid-thirties to early forties. They were uniformly thin and lanky. Jim Henry wondered again, as he often had, why so many of the male operatives in the mill seemed cut from the same mold.

The constable pretended not to notice a mason jar one of the men was hastily putting under his chair.

"Evenin' boys, not a happy time for a gatherin' is it?"

"I reckon not," one of the men murmured.

"You had yore supper, Jim Henry?" another asked. "They's plenty in the kitchen."

The constable pulled a chair around so he sat facing the men. "Maybe I'll have a bite in a minute. Right now I'm wonderin' if any of you boys could help me figure out who shot yer buddy here. I know he did rub right many people the wrong way."

There was general laughter as one of the men drawled, "I reckon he rubbed more'n a few women the right way though."

"Well," Jim Henry replied, "tell me more about that. I hear he had a row with somebody a week ago Saturday night, and that row started about some woman."

"They wuz a row all right," said one of the men. "I seen it myself. Ever body laughin', tellin' jokes and havin' a good time, but next thing you know Snag pops the hell out of ole Rafer. Then Rafe storms outta there and comes back in with a gun. He's aimin' to kill Snag sure as hell, but his pistol misfires. Then Snag beat Rafer like a drum."

Another man volunteered, "You know Rafer doffs warps with ole Ed Crocker—them things weigh three hundred pound or so—and he can't lift his end of 'em now cause his ribs is broke up and he hurts just getting outta a chair. If his wife didn't work I don't know what Rafe would do."

Jim Henry waited to see if more information would be forthcoming. When there was none he said, "I appreciate you tellin' me about that. I'm gonna talk to Rafer. But what about this woman thing?"

"Don't rightly know," another man said. "All I heard was Snag say, 'You ain't a man 'til you do.' Then Rafer said something and Snag popped him."

Jim Henry made several more attempts to get information that might be helpful, but to no avail, so he went into the kitchen to visit with the women who were there.

In the kitchen, a table was very nearly covered with food. Neighbors did not express sympathy, nor note a passing, through flowers; instead they brought food. The three women sitting around the table were of various ages and various builds—one very heavy, one very thin and the third just a bit chubby. Unlike the uniformly lanky village men, the women seemed to be a great deal more varied in body type.

The kitchen was so small that it was almost filled by the iron wood stove, the table and the women—so much so that Jim Henry had trouble getting into the room.

"How are you ladies?" he asked.

"Right wore out," one of them replied. "Six to six with a spinnin' frame don't leave a body much to go on."

"Have a bite to eat, Jim Henry," said another. "They's right good macaroni and cheese, and they's a spot of tater salad left, what them in the front room didn't wolf down. You see all the cake and pie. People surely do bring sweets to a wake."

The constable refused the food. He thought it likely these women would know nothing of use about Snag, still he asked, "Do any of you have any ideas about who might have shot Snag?"

"You might ought to look on The Line," one woman volunteered. "Our colored folks didn't hold with Snag and his ways."

"Why was that?"

The women looked at each other. After a moment one volunteered, "Well he was knowed to chase women. That's the cause of his wife leavin'—that and him drinkin' and gamblin' away all his pay—and he mighta been foolin' with one of them young colored girls."

The other women nodded their assent.

As Jim Henry walked home he thought, women likely see more and know more than we men seem to expect. Those old hens just might have hit the nail on the head. But if the killer turns out to be from The Line there'll be hell to pay—might even have to try to hold off a lynching. He hoped June was right and nobody on The Line had shot Snag.

DAY TWO

Jim Henry slept late the next day. That is to say, he rose at six thirty instead of five thirty. At seven he sat down to a large plate of sausage along with hot biscuits covered in thick gravy made of milk, butter, flour, and scrapings from the bottom of the pan in which the sausage had been fried. Joann sat opposite eating a biscuit covered with molasses.

"I remembered somethin' important last night," Jim Henry said. "I remembered that you women have yore own gossip circles, and you generally don't let us men know what you hear, or what you see."

"Probably we see what's right there in front of us, and in front of you. But you men don't see much of anything," Joann replied. "You just sort of blunder through life—thinking about your jobs, and your hunting, and your fishing, and bragging about yourselves."

Jim Henry smiled, "Well that's as may be. But tell me what you and the old biddies know about Snag Wiley."

"The same thing you know, Snag was a tom cat. He was good for nothing but to drink, gamble, and go a-whoring."

"I know, I know. That's generally true, but do you hear anything about him and some woman in the village? I begin to think he might've been seein' some respectable woman here about."

"Respectable? No respectable woman would be in the same room with Snag unless her husband or some of her male kin was with her."

"Well, okay, but you know what I'm sayin'—some woman we all think of as respectable then. What I mean is, could he have been seein' some woman whose husband, or brother, or daddy took exception to 'im?"

Joann chuckled, "Indeed, 'Took exception to him?' That's a pretty round about way to say they blew a hole in him. If he and some woman were messing around like you say, then they were being awfully careful. I've got no wind of it."

Jim Henry ate for a moment. "But still—maybe there's some widder woman who's missin' having a man around. Or maybe some young girl got an itch to experiment. It does happen you know."

"Well," said Joann, "you men like to think there's a whole world full of women like that out there. But if there is, I don't see them in Boiling Springs."

"What if it was one of our coloreds," asked Jim Henry. "Is that more likely?"

"Shame on you! I know, and you know, there are colored women who make their living doing such, 'cause they can't live any other way. But our coloreds are good God fearing, family people. I don't see any of their women with the likes of Snag Wiley either."

There was a knocking at the back door, and Jim Henry could see a young black boy standing looking into the kitchen. He got up and walked to the door. "Mornin' boy—what can I do for you?"

The boy looked up. "Mr. Jim Henry, Mr. Harry wants to know could you stop by the store. And could you do it right soon? He say it's important. He say he needs to talk to you."

Harry Simmons was manager of the company store.

"Okay son, you tell Mr. Harry I'll be along directly."

Jim Henry returned to the kitchen table. "Harry must be riled about somethin'. I'm surprised he's at the store this early. I wonder if Forrest Hames has tied a knot in his young nephew's tail."

"It would surprise me if Mr. Hames was not riding him pretty hard. I'm sure he gave Harry that job because he was kin, but he won't keep him if he doesn't measure up. Do you think he will?"

"Measure up you mean? Well, Harry does spend money foolish like. But most young folks do. I do wonder though if he's sound enough when it comes to managin' his uncle's store." Jim Henry shook his head, "I just don't know how he'll turn out. I bet Mr. Hames is pushin' him hard." The constable chuckled, "But that ole man pushes ever body hard."

* * *

The company store dominated the town square and it was Forrest Hames' pride and joy. As it was the largest and most complete general store for miles around, the villagers took pride in it as well. The store occupied the ground floor and basement of a two story brick building that was approximately one hundred by one hundred feet. The street level front of the building contained large plate glass display windows. Upon entering the front center door, piece goods, notions and ladies' ready-to-wear were to one's right. On the left were men's shoes and clothing. To the far left was the drug department. The rear of the store contained a small ice cream parlor and a millinery department, with a resident milliner who had been brought in from Baltimore. There were two millinery "openings" each year, and these were social as well as merchandising events. The milliner's good looks and big city, sophisticated air made the village men especially eager to accompany their wives or sisters to these openings.

The store basement was shared by the grocery and hardware departments. Harry Simmons' office was on the second floor next to the doctor's office. The town hall was also on the second floor, as was a large room used as a lodge hall for the Odd Fellows, the Red Men, and the Knights of Pythias. Simmons was a member of the Red Men, and held the post of Noble Grand in the Odd Fellows.

As Jim Henry entered Simmons' office he was greeted by Eula Morgan, who served as both bookkeeper for the store and secretary for the manager. "Good morning constable, Mr. Simmons is expecting you. Just go on in."

"Mornin' Miss Eula, hope you're well. Yes, I see Harry's door's open."

As Jim Henry walked in, Simmons rose, came around his desk, and closed the office door behind the constable. The store manager was in his early thirties, short and tending toward being rotund. This morning he was clearly agitated.

"Jim Henry, I'm in a peck of trouble. You've got to help me out."

Jim Henry turned and looked at his friend. "Harry, what's got you so riled? I thought a man who'd just bought a fine pair of horses and a fancy buggy would be feeling pretty much on topa the world."

Harry threw up his hands. "Don't you go raggin' on me, Jim Henry. Fancy rigs ain't gonna mean a thing to me 'less I can find out who's stealin' from the store."

Simmons and Jim Henry sat down in the two chairs located in front of the manager's desk.

"Okay Harry, tell me what's goin' on."

"Jim Henry, we just finished an inventory and it looks like they's been near eighty dollars stole from the store. I'm gonna have to make that up and try to keep Uncle Forrest from findin' out about the theft. If he learns they's been stealin' right from under my nose I'll be back on the farm before you can say 'Jack Robinson.'"

"When did this stealin' take place?" Jim Henry asked.

"That's part of the problem. I don't know. I didn't know anything was wrong until we just finished inventory. We have records of the goods we buy for the store. We also have records of what's been sold, and of course with the inventory we know what we have in stock. Now in several places the items sold plus the items on hand don't add up to the items we brought in. They's a few items missin' here and a few items missin' there and it all adds up to seventy seven dollars and fifteen cents. For some of the hands in the mill that would be near three months wages, or more. It ain't quite that for me, but it's a lot."

Jim Henry waited for Harry to say more. When he did not the

constable asked, "You think folks're walkin' out with stuff without payin' for it?"

"I wouldn't usually reckon so," Simmons replied. "We got lotsa clerks and they watch folks like a hawk."

"But one of the clerks coulda been in cahoots with somebody, and let 'em walk out with things?"

"You see that's what makes it so bad. Any way you look at it, it's one of our help that's doing the stealin'; or they're in on it somehow."

"If people ain't walkin' out with stuff, is they any other way you can look at it?"

"Well, some clerk could just be pocketin' money. So a thing could be sold you see, but not show up as sold."

"How could that happen, Harry?"

Simmons squirmed in his seat. After a short time he said, "It could be like this. Ever sale is wrote up on a ticket; that ticket's stuck on a spindle beside whatever cash box the money goes in, and the customer gets a copy. But half the folks coming in here can't read, and they don't want a ticket no how. So if a clerk were of a mind to, ever now and then they could just not write up an item and stick the money in their pocket."

"But Harry, don't the clerks watch one another?"

"I thought so, but maybe they don't, 'cause that's a real possible way the stealin' could be done."

Jim Henry looked at his shoes and he and Harry sat silent. There might be another way, Jim Henry thought. Miss Eula just might be involved. Did she have access to the cash after it had left the store below? She certainly had access to all the sales slips that had been written. But there was some talk that Harry and Eula were more than just employer and employee. Maybe it was best not to go down that road just yet.

"Does the theft seem to be just in one department? Or do we hafta suspect all the store help?"

Harry sighed. "It ain't as bad as all that. Most of the missin' items—I mean items not showin' up as sold—are in the men's department. But they's a few in hardware, a few in drugs, and a few in notions. It's just little things. It's things like long johns or socks in men's wear, thread or scissors in notions, and lotion or rubbin' alcohol in drugs."

"So, of them clerkin' in the men's department do you suspect one more than another?"

"I don't think so. You know they's Hoyle, Rat Tail, and Byron. I trust 'em all—or they'd not be working in the store. But I guess one of 'em might just have to be involved. Still, they's them items from other departments."

Hoyle Kendrick's old enough to be a father to both Byron and Rat Tail, Jim Henry thought. He's a deacon in the Baptist Church and well respected by everyone. Rat Tail don't enjoy the same reputation as Hoyle, but he's still not one you would suspect of theft. Byron's considered by all to be honest.

Byron was a Scruggs and a younger brother of Amos, who would be busy burying Snag Wiley in a short while. This reminded Jim Henry that he was planning to attend that burying.

"Harry, I'm gonna have to git back to you on this. I want to go up to the cemetery and see Snag put in the ground. All I can think of right now is that you might do more floor walkin'."

"Well, for God's sake don't forget about this. I need to find out who's behind this stealin' before some word of it leaks out to Uncle Forrest. This has to be kept quiet."

* * *

The cemetery in Boiling Springs lay about one hundred yards northeast of the livery stable. When Jim Henry arrived there the body had not yet arrived, nor did he see the minister. There were only a half dozen of Snag's buddies standing around a freshly opened grave. A few dozen yards away, in the shade of a tree, sat the three black men who had dug the grave. Actually the three men were more brown than black and all had the thin, lanky build that was predominant among the village males. Mose Little, the oldest of the three, was also the pastor of the black church, a stone mason and an accomplished musician, on both fiddle and banjo. The younger men, R. D. Jones and Gaston Foster were day laborers who were irregular and infrequent employees of the furniture store.

Jim Henry walked over to chat with the diggers.

"Mornin' Mose, R. D., Gaston. You boys must've been workin' before it was good light."

Mose answered, "Yes sir, Cap'n. After a man git down in that dirt about one and a half foot they's nothin' but red clay. That makes for hard diggin'."

"Is Preacher Tarleton gonna speak over Mr. Snag?" Gaston asked.

"I think so Gaston, but probably you know as much about that as I do."

"If he do," Gaston said, "I expect it'll be 'bout like a story I heard."

"How's that?"

"Well, this man and his brother wuz real rounders—into ever sort of devilment you ever heard of. Now the one man died, and his brother went to the preacher and said he'd pay him fifty dollars if he'd speak over his brother and say he was a saint." Gaston grinned, "Would you believe that preacher said he would do it?"

Jim Henry chuckled, "Come on, Gaston!"

"No sir, Cap'n. It's the truth."

"I just bet it is."

Gaston continued, "Well, word got out. The whole country turned up at the grave to hear that preacher lie, like he'd said he'd do. So the preacher, he stands up over the corpse and he says, 'Here before us is the body of a man who lied, cheated, stole and went a-whorin'. He was the worst sort of a scoundrel. But compared to his brother he was a saint.'"

Mose grinned and shook his head. The other men chuckled.

"You and me can set here and laugh," said Mose. "But we talkin' serious now about Mr. Snag. I am shore thankful I ain't in his place."

Gaston chimed in, "I shore am glad 'bout that too." R. D. just nodded.

Mose continued, "And I ain't talking just 'bout bein' dead. That man is right now facing judgment. I ain't 'bout to take the Lord's place and say how that judgment is goin'. But I'm shorely glad I'm not in his place."

John Henry nodded and said, "Mose, you're a mighty kind and generous man. Some on The Line, and some white folks too, already passed judgment on ole Snag. That judgment's not in his favor neither."

R. D. never said much, for he had a pronounced stutter. But at this point he joined in. "Tha..tha..that Mr. Snag was pure..pure..purely mean. And he wa...he wa..he was meaner with black folks that he was with wh..wh..white."

"'Scuse me for sayin' so Mr. Jim Henry," said Gaston, "but R. D. done spoke the truth."

"I won't argue with R. D.," Jim Henry said. "I'm glad I'm not in Snag's place, but I'm glad I'm not in Rev. Tarleton's place neither. I couldn't think of anything to say over ole Snag that would be fittin'."

* * *

A wagon came up Main Street from the south, and turned east past the Baptist Church toward the cemetery. Amos Scruggs was driving, a black man was seated beside him, and in the bed of the wagon was the coffin of Snag Wiley. Rev. Tarleton must have been in the church yard waiting for Amos, because as the wagon passed the church, he fell in behind it. Tarleton was a tall, clean cut young man recently graduated from Wake Forest College. The young women liked him, for he was single. But village opinion was not all in the Reverend's favor. He was suspected of holding to a theology that bore the taint of liberalism, although villagers would not, perhaps could not, have expressed their concern in just that way.

The wagon stopped beside the open grave and Amos' black assistant jumped down and took two heavy boards from the wagon. These were placed across the grave. Next, lengths of rope were laid across each board, with several feet of rope coiled on either side of the grave. The black man then joined Mose, Gaston and R. D. in the shade. Amos selected four of the men standing by to take the coffin (a very cheap, crude, wooden box with two rope handles on each side) off the wagon and place it on the boards spanning the grave. Jim Henry had walked over to the grave site, arriving shortly after Rev. Tarleton.

Rev. Tarleton greeted each of the men by name and shook their hand. He then said a short prayer, and began, "We are here today to bury Zebulon Wiley."

The minister looked at the coffin and there was a long silence—so long that Jim Henry thought the preacher would not continue. But he did.

"The death of a family member, friend, or acquaintance is always a time of sorrow. That is normal. But sometimes that sorrow is tempered. If the departed is old and infirm, or has been long ill, our sorrow is diminished by the knowledge that he has been relieved of pain and suffering. Most of all however, if the deceased is a Christian, then sorrow is mixed with the joy that comes from knowing Jesus has welcomed home one of his beloved children."

Again there was a long pause. "We are especially sorrowful at the death of our brother Zebulon, for we do not have the assurance that he has entered heaven. We hope so much, and we pray so much, that he has." Again there was a pause.

"We cannot see into a man's soul. We do not know the state of Zebulon's soul at the moment he drew his last breath."

Here the pastor looked around and smiled at those gathered around the grave. "But we can each of us see to our own soul. For however much we might wish it otherwise, however much we may push the thought away, we know that each of us must face death. And friends, we should all see to it that on that day—that day we know will come—those gathered around *our* grave will know with great certainty that we are walking the golden streets of paradise." Here again there was a pause as the pastor looked at each of the men around the grave. Then he continued, "And what must we do to gain heaven at the end? It is so simple, my friends and neighbors. We must only come to the cross of Jesus and put our trust in Him. Then at that hour when our life on earth is over we will face not just an end, but a glorious beginning."

The pastor stood looking at the coffin. He then said, "May God have mercy on the soul of Zebulon Wiley."

After another prayer Rev. Tarleton indicated that the burial should proceed. The pastor began walking back to the church and the men around the grave began to disperse. Amos waved the four black men over. Each man took a grip on an end of one of the ropes, and at a signal from Amos they pulled on the ropes and lifted the coffin a bit. Amos removed the boards that had been supporting the casket and the men slowly lowered it into the ground. Then the ropes were pulled out from one side, coiled, and placed in the wagon along with the boards.

Amos and his helper drove away as the three gravediggers began to close the grave. None of the others remained except Jim Henry.

After the black men had been working for a time Jim Henry took Mose aside and spoke softly in hopes the other two men could not hear. "Mose, you bein' a preacher and all, you know most ever thing that happens on The Line, and I bet you know what's goin' on in the rest of the village too."

Mose reacted with surprise at the implied secrecy. But he replied in a similar low tone, "Mr. Jim Henry, I just know what the peoples tell me. I don't ask folks to tell me they troubles, and I surely don't ask 'em to tell me 'bout other folks. But they do tell me. They tell me right much."

"Then maybe you know something about Snag Wiley and some woman on The Line."

Mose shook his head and took a short step back, "Mr. Jim Henry, ain't nobody on The Line had no truck with Mr. Snag—far as I know anyway. I think the sisters on The Line would as soon consort with a black snake as with Mr. Snag."

"But Mose..." Jim Henry began; then he stopped. Maybe Mose was right. Maybe no black woman was involved. He smiled, "But nothin' I reckon, Mose. I'll leave you boys to it."

Addressing all three men the constable said, "Be careful now. That sun's mighty hot, and you boys don't want to be in no grave, 'less you're diggin' it for somebody else. Ain't that right?"

Gaston chuckled and said, "That is the truth Cap'n."

Jim Henry decided it was time for his talk with Rafer Jones.

* * *

Rafer's house was on the east edge of the village and not too far from the cemetery. As the constable approached, he saw Rafer sitting under a huge Chinaberry tree that grew in front of the house. When building of the village had begun, the village area had been stripped bare. But this tree had clearly been spared. For the Chinaberry could not have grown so large in eight years, nor even in twenty eight years.

Rafer wore faded overalls with no shirt and Jim Henry could see his midsection was heavily taped. One eye was still swollen almost shut and one side of Rafer's face was a rainbow of yellows, purples, and black. From the careful way he was drinking a glass of sweet tea, it was apparent his lips and mouth had been badly cut and were not yet completely healed.

"Hello Rafer. I've seen you lookin' better. You gettin' yore beauty sleep?"

In a tone of disgust Rafer said, "Well Jim Henry, it only hurts when I laugh. Thank God you didn't say nothin' funny."

"Sorry Rafer. I heard all about what happened. I really am right sorry." The constable sighed, "But you know somebody done a whole lot worse to Snag. And I reckon you know lots of folks think it was you who shot the ole son."

Rafer snorted, "If you've heard all about it, you know I tried my best to shoot 'im." He sat quietly for a time, shook his head and said,

"I've thought right much about me tryin' to shoot that son of a bitch. I don't know if I'm glad my piece of shit pistol misfired or not. First I thought I was glad I didn't kill 'im; 'cause if I had I'da hung, or gone to jail forever. But now I think I'm gonna take the blame for killin' 'im anyway—without the satisfaction of doin' it."

"You won't take the blame for it if you didn't do it."

"You don't know that!"

The constable had to admit that was true. But to Rafer he said, "You and Snag were buddies. How come he hit you and started all that row?"

"So you don't know all about it, do you?"

"Okay, I guess I don't. But I know the important part. I just don't know who the female in question was. Oh! And another thing, I don't know why you didn't keep your mouth shut when Snag said, 'You're not a man 'til you do.'"

Rafer shook his head again. "I don't know who the colored gal is neither."

Jim Henry showed no sign he had learned something new. He merely nodded and waited to see if Rafer would continue.

After painfully taking a sip of his tea Rafer went on, "I just said to Snag that I'd heard he was screwin' some colored gal. He looked kinda sheepish, you know, but he said, 'You know what they say 'bout screwin' colored gals—you're not a man 'til you do.' And I reckon I said, 'But when you do, then you're a son of a bitch.'"

Rafer took another sip of tea, and continued, "How'd I know he wouldn't just laugh at that? I reckon he was on edge about somethin' and that just struck him wrong."

Both men sat silent for a time. Finally Rafer said, "Weren't no call for Snag to act the way he did. When he hit me I just went sorta crazy. You know what happened then. I can't say I'm all that sorry he's dead, but I didn't kill Snag. That's the God's truth, Jim Henry."

Jim Henry knew that sometimes men react in foolish ways. He'd seen too much violence that was due to alcohol. He'd also seen violence that was due to stress, or humiliation, or the weather. He knew that if Snag had had one less drink, or if it had been a bit cooler, or if any one of a number of apparently insignificant things had been different, Snag might have slapped Rafer on the back and laughed. Then Rafer would be at work today. But would Snag be alive, or would he still be dead and buried?

"I've gotta ask Rafer, you have a shotgun?"

"Well hell fire Jim Henry, of course I got a shotgun. Who do you know who don't have one?"

"I think I'd better have a look at it."

"You just go in the back bedroom and git it then. It's on the wall over the bed. I ain't hobbling in there with my ribs complainin' all the way."

Jim Henry returned with the shotgun. "It's a twelve gauge; and Rafer, it looks like it's been fired pretty recent."

"Hell yes! My old lady got it last night to shoot a copperhead she saw by the outhouse. I don't clean a gun ever single time it's fired. But if I'd killed Snag with it I'd sure as hell see that it was clean when you come nosin' around, now wouldn't I?"

"Or you'd be sly enough to not clean it just so you could use that argument."

"Good God all mighty, Jim Henry! Nobody ever accused me of being that smart. I'm telling you I just plain did not shoot Zebulon 'Snag' Wiley. Now go find another pore sufferin' soul to torment and let me set here and feel sorry for myself."

Jim Henry thought Rafer made a good point. So he smiled and said, "Alright Rafer, I'm sorry I have to trouble you, but you gotta know I'm probably not through with you yet. You take care, and I hope you can git back to work soon."

With that Jim Henry returned the shotgun to its rack and headed toward his home—with thoughts of beans and greens. His having been called away earlier to confer with the company store manager had kept him from some planned weeding in the early morning cool. Now he thought he would tend his garden a bit before the heat became even more oppressive.

But the garden, as it turned out, would have to wait. As Jim Henry reached Main Street, he was hailed by Forrest Hames, who had just stepped into the street from his yard.

"Constable, I was just about to have my house man hunt you up. I'm glad I ran into you. Walk with me to my office; I want to hear what progress you've made."

"I can tell you in a few words. They's one suspect that I know, and another suspect I don't know."

"I'm sure there's more. And I want to know that more. But let's not talk about it on the street."

* * *

The building that housed the offices of Boiling Springs Mills sat on the south edge of the town square, facing north. Hames' private office was in the northeast corner of the building. As the men entered, Hames indicated Jim Henry should take a seat in front of the massive desk. Hames then moved a second chair aside so he could move around and seat himself behind the desk.

Jim Henry wondered if Hames really felt a need to assert his position in this obvious way. He didn't know if he should feel slighted or amused. He merely sat and looked at Hames.

"Well, speak up. Who is this suspect you know? And how can you have a suspect you don't know?"

"First off Mr. Hames, it seems Snag beat Rafer Jones near 'bout to a pulp a week ago this past Saturday night. The fracas started because of a comment Rafer made. Snag smacked him; then Rafer went for his pistol and tried to kill Snag, but his revolver misfired."

Hames snapped, "Where did this fight take place?"

"South of here, across the state line. They's a little beer joint over there lotsa the men visit."

"And Rafer was not the one who started the fight?"

"That's what I've been told."

Hames leaned back in his chair. He looked at the ceiling, then back at the constable. "Hmmm. Well, I guess if the fight wasn't on company property I'll not worry about that. Not right now anyway. So you suspect Jones?"

"Since he tried to kill Snag once, and Snag beat 'im without mercy, it might be he tried again and succeeded. So yes, Rafer's got to be a suspect."

"But how likely do you think it is that Rafer's the one?"

"I think they's less than a fifty-fifty chance Rafer killed Snag. Snag was likely shot down by the river, and Rafer's in such bad shape he would've had a hard time walkin' that far. But then again they's no proof one way or another. No witnesses. Hell fire, far as I know now nobody even heard a shot, nor a ruckus of any sort."

Hames snapped, "I've told you constable, watch your language."

Jim Henry took a deep breath and raised his eyes to the ceiling. But he made no comment.

"Now, what's this about a suspect you don't know?"

"Here's how that goes. It's pretty certain Snag was, well, let's say cavortin' with one of the gals from The Line. Since that's the case, I figure a husband, a daddy, or maybe a brother of this gal might've shot him. But since I don't know which colored gal it was, I don't know who might've sent Snag to his reward—if reward it was."

Jim Henry couldn't remember a time when Forrest Hames had looked frightened, but he came very near looking frightened now.

"Constable, it can't be somebody from The Line killed Snag. It just can't be!"

Taken aback, Jim Henry slowly replied, "Well ... it might not be; but then again it might." Hames seemed to take no notice, so the constable continued. "Folks on The Line are just folks, like ever body else. They git mad. They shoot up one another and cut one another up. I reckon they might shoot up one of us white folks."

Hames moved a paperweight on his desk, then fiddled with a stack of papers. Finally he looked out the window and said, "I'm planning to hire a few coloreds to work in the mill, well not really *in* the mill, but opening cotton bales and moving the cotton on into the card room. That's going to be a little touchy." Looking at the constable he continued, "You might not know it, but operatives in a South Carolina mill near here walked out some months ago when a few coloreds were hired on. To get them back to work the super had to issue a statement to the effect that the coloreds would be let go and no others would be hired. If somebody from The Line has killed Snag, our folks surely won't accept coloreds working in the mill."

Jim Henry waited for Hames to say more, but he did not.

"I see," Jim Henry said. "Well, yes, I admit, they could be trouble." After a moment he added, "I like to think our folks are more level headed than them sand lappers. But they was that lynchin' in Forest City not so many years back—nineteen hundred I believe it was."

Hames stood up and Jim Henry knew he was being dismissed.

"What's done is done. Even prayer won't change that. But until you know for sure who shot Snag don't you let on to anybody that we might've had one of our coloreds kill a white man."

As the constable turned to leave the office Hames said, "You hear me constable?"

Jim Henry did not reply. He knew full well word would come out. He himself had raised the question of Snag's possible shenanigans with a black woman while talking with Mose. And Rafer could not be forced to keep quiet. Worse yet, it would occur to Rafer before long, if it had not already, that a good way to direct suspicion away from himself was to direct suspicion toward The Line. It was clear that he'd best discover the name of the black woman as soon as possible.

* * *

Jim Henry needed to talk to Mose again. The black minister could possibly identify the woman Snag had been with, and he could be trusted to keep that identity secret. When Jim Henry arrived back at the cemetery Snag's grave had been refilled; Mose and Gaston were gone and R. D. was walking away in the direction of The Line. Jim Henry hailed the grave digger and hurried to catch up to him. "R. D. I'm lookin' for Mose. Where'd he go?"

"Mm.. Mm.. Mose done gone over to wh... wh... where Mr. Broadus buildin' hisself a new house. Mose lay.. lay.. lay.. layin' stone for the foundation. He ain't bu... bu... been gone but a few m..m..minutes."

"Thanks R. D."

Jim Henry immediately turned back toward the cemetery. Broadus White had bought some land just a quarter mile or so outside the village and east of the cemetery. There Mose would be laying stone. It was likely, the constable thought, he would get but little from Mose. And any information he did get would not come quickly. Mose had been sincere in his earlier comment; he truly could not imagine one of the women on The Line with Snag. So, Jim Henry wondered, after talking with Mose, what should be the next step? He honestly did not know.

* * *

At first Jim Henry thought R. D. had been mistaken. At the new home site he saw only piles of lumber and stone, and the beginnings of a stone foundation. There was no sign of Mose, or anyone else. But as he looked around, he saw Mose with two buckets of water coming up hill from the nearby creek. As yet there had been no well dug for the new house.

Mose set his buckets of water beside the tin lined wooden trough in which he would mix mortar for his stone work. He grinned at Jim Henry.

"Cap'n. I didn't know you wuz follerin' me around today."

"Well, I didn't start out to, Mose. But I've learned somethin' since we spoke, and now I need to ask you to do a favor for me."

"Yes sir. What's that?"

"In spite of what you told me just a while ago, they is a black woman that Snag was, well, screwin'. Most likely that woman is from The Line. Mose, I really need to know who she is. You're the person who can find her out."

Mose shook his head, "I can't believe you're right, Mr. Jim Henry. Mr. Snag was a bad 'un. I can't see none of the sisters with him."

"I know, I know, but I got it almost from the horse's mouth. Snag was screwin' a colored gal. She might not be from The Line, but most likely she is. That word's gonna get out, and when it does people will think somebody from The Line killed Snag. Now Mose, you know as well as I do that might spark a fire we don't want. If it wasn't this girl's kin—or boy friend—that shot Snag, I need to prove that quick as I can. If it was, I need to lock that boy away right quick. That's the only way I see I can keep things from getting' outta hand, and ugly as hell."

Mose stood looking down at his mixing trough. He sighed deeply and looked off over the creek.

"Cap'n, I think you may be right 'bout they bein' trouble. I don't know if I can help you. But I'll see what I can find out."

"I do thank you, Mose. I'll not let nobody know where I learned whatever you tell me."

Mose took out his knife, cut open a bag of cement, picked up the bag and emptied it into the mixing trough. He then added water from one of the buckets, picked up a hoe, and with it mixed the mortar a little. Mose stopped and looked at the mixture. He then added a bit more water and continued to mix.

For a while Jim Henry quietly watched the black man mixing mortar. Finally he said, "One more thing Mose, if you got any ideas how I ought to go about findin' Snag's killer—on or off The Line—you let me know. I'm pretty well stumped."

Mose looked briefly at Jim Henry, shook his head, and continued working his hoe through the contents of the mixing trough.

* * *

Joann had been ironing most all morning, but now she sat at her writing desk and wondered if there was not something more she could say in her account of the first ever murder in Boiling Springs.

The writing desk was Joann's proudest possession. Her family had not always been "dirt poor mountain folk," and the desk had been built especially for her great grandfather in Lancaster, Pennsylvania. It had then been brought down the Great Wagon Road, through Salisbury, and on to Charlotte by her grandfather in 1856. In Charlotte, with the aid of bad judgment, bad luck, and the Civil War, grandfather had managed to bring the family into, perhaps genteel, but near total, poverty. A few dozen books and the writing desk were among the very few things saved as the family moved to the mountains some three dozen or so miles north of the spot where Boiling Springs would later be built.

When she heard Jim Henry at the door Joann called, "Come talk to me about Snag's murder. Surely I can say something more than his body was found on the dam. Can't I say there's a suspect?"

Jim Henry came and propped himself on a corner of the large desk. "No, I'd sure rather you not say they's a suspect. If you do the folks at the paper'll want you to say who it is and why. I feel like that'd do nobody good. Some of my thinkin's gonna get out soon enough without the newspaper helpin' things along."

"Okay, but if it's going to get out anyway why—?"

"What've you got for a body to eat?"

Joann threw up her hands, sighed, and stood. "Oh all right! You probably could have been here to eat when I was expecting you. But yes, of course I've got some food ready. I've been waiting on you."

As she put out their lunch on the kitchen table Joann asked, "Are you thinking Rafer's the one that killed Snag?"

"I don't rightly know. He could be, but it might be one of our coloreds. Seems pretty certain Snag was messin' with some woman over there on The Line."

"Oh I hope not."

"I sure do too."

The couple began their meal and ate in silence for a time. Then Jim Henry sighed and said, "It ain't real clear what I ought to do next."

* * *

The river that powered the Boiling Springs cotton mill was crossed by a bridge located just below the dam, and just above the mouth of Puzzle Creek. Jim Henry now guided his horse onto the bridge. After lunch he had decided he should ride over the state line to the beer parlor where Snag had fought with Rafer.

The level of the bridge was somewhat below the top of the dam, but on the west side of the river the road rose quickly and soon the constable could look across the mill pond to the Boiling Springs textile plant. As he rode along he could just make out a hum floating across the water from the plant. It was, he was sure, the noise of the looms in the weave room.

Over the bridge, on the west side of the river, there were eight mill houses, all on the south side of the road. Except for these houses, the entire mill village was located on the east side of the river. But Boiling Springs Mills had more enterprises than the mill, mill village and company store. Company farms were located on both sides of the river. And beyond the eight mill houses, as the road turned somewhat to the south, Jim Henry rode for about two miles passing nothing but company farms. Then, crossing a second river, he rode past independent farms for another two miles or so to the state line.

Not even a hundred yards over the state line was the beer parlor that catered largely to those refugees from the dry North Carolina county in which Boiling Springs was located. The establishment was named, with total lack of imagination, The State Line. The State Line was not an impressive structure. It was a rectangular wooden building measuring not more than fifteen by thirty feet. Inside there was a bar and four tables. When Jim Henry entered there were only three men in the building, including the bartender. As he was eyed suspiciously, he identified himself immediately.

"Afternoon boys. I'm the constable over in Boiling Springs. An ole boy who was a good customer here's been killed and I'm tryin' to find out who might've done it."

The bartender's reply did not bode well.

"If you're constable in Boiling Springs you got no authority here."

"Well, that's right. But it don't matter, 'cause I'm not gonna try to enforce no law while I'm here. I just come in to talk."

"Trouble is, even if you're just talking you're likely to scare off my customers."

"No reason I should, but anyway I'll leave right quick after you tell me about who might've had reason to shoot Snag Wiley."

One of the customers chuckled and shook his head. Jim Henry turned to the man and asked, "You know somethin' I oughta hear?"

After taking a long drink of his beer the customer said, "I bet you know he beat hell outta Rafer Jones. I expect ole Rafe had right much reason."

"That's what I heard. I ain't real sure Rafer's the one shot Snag though. Maybe I ain't even a little bit sure. I was wonderin' if they was anybody else."

The bartender apparently decided he'd try to hurry Jim Henry's departure. Leaning on the bar he said, "Snag was a rough 'un. They's more than a few he's had a ruckus with. But ain't nobody but Rafer he's smacked around lately."

"Well, who has he smacked around—not lately?"

Now the second customer spoke up. "Come on constable. For the past half dozen or so years, since that mill over yonder opened up, Snag's been comin' in here drinkin' and carryin' on. Right off he sorta become the cock of the walk."

"And?"

"And ever now and then some young buck'd decide to test ole Snag. They'd start raggin' on him and they might even git a lick in at Snag, but if they did he'd usually floor 'em. 'Course I don't believe he ever beat somebody like he beat Rafer."

"Anybody try to shoot him before?"

"Well, no. They ain't been nobody tried that. Not that I've knowed of."

The four men stood silent for a time. Then the bartender said, "Them young 'uns was testin' their selves more'n they was testin' Snag. And Snag never held no grudge. I don't believe any of them boys he fought with held one neither."

Jim Henry chuckled, "You boys tellin' me that nobody took exception to Snag whoppin' 'em, except maybe Rafer? Is that it?"

"Sounds pretty weak don't it?" the bartender asked. "But I believe that's the way of it. I don't remember Snag havin' no trouble for months now. If it was one of them others why would they wait so long to shoot him? I just ain't gonna sic you on none of them fellers."

Jim Henry waited to see if anyone had anything to add. It became obvious they did not.

"Well, I don't know that you boys helped me out a lot. But I appreciate you talkin' with me. I don't think I give you my name. I'm Jim Henry Tate and if you learn anything about who killed yer drinkin' buddy I sure hope you'll let me know."

* * *

Over dinner Jim Henry told Joann about his visit to The State Line. "It's kind of funny," she said. "It sounds like something from a dime novel about the old west. You know, where there's this old gunfighter who's the very best and all the young ones just have to try him out."

"I didn't think of that. 'Course you're the reader. I don't git much past the newspaper."

"But you don't think any of the 'young guns' might have killed Snag?"

"I don't think it's worth my time to go down that road. And even if I did I don't know how I'd get the names of them fellers."

"So you've got Rafer."

"I don't think Rafer could've done it. I got nobody."

"What about somebody on The Line?"

"They is that. I druther have nobody though."

DAY THREE

Wednesday was cool and cloudy and Jim Henry was early in his garden. First he used his little push plow to turn under the weeds between the rows of plants. Next he pulled by hand those weeds that were so close to the roots of his tomatoes and beans that the plow could not reach them. Then he pulled the weeds hiding under the turnip greens, and scattered guano—the villagers' most popular fertilizer. Finally he picked the few tomatoes that were ripe.

By eight fifteen the constable was sitting on his back porch steps drinking that second cup of coffee he had not allowed himself at breakfast. He heard some conversation drifting from the front porch. This was followed by a young man coming around the house and asking, "Are you Constable Jim Henry Tate?"

"I have to admit I am."

"Well, here's a warrant for the arrest of Joe Kenny."

"Hah! I bet it's for sellin' whiskey ain't it?"

"Yes sir, constable, I reckon it is."

"Now don't think I ain't knowed what Joe was up to, but I never caught him red handed, and nobody was gonna admit he sold 'em their whiskey. But how come they got proof of his dealin' at the county seat, and I don't? "

The young man grinned. "It seems a feller from east of here a ways was sellin' whiskey awful cheap in our colored section. He was offerin' five gallon kegs for five dollars each."

"That sounds too cheap."

"Yeah it does, and it wuz. Anyway, some colored boys sampled the stuff and collected what money they could and struck a bargain. They offered eight seventy five for two kegs and the seller took their offer."

"I'll be!"

"But don't you know, when them coloreds tried to divide up the whiskey they couldn't get but a pint outta each keg—even though they could hear it sloshin' around in there."

"How 'bout that!"

"Well, when them boys took the heads off the kegs they saw they'd been snookered. Each keg had a pint bottle of whiskey fastened to the bung hole and the rest of the keg was filled with water. Right clever trick I figure."

Jim Henry chuckled, "It is devious. But how'd that turn out a warrant for Joe Kenny?"

"One of them coloreds knew the man that gypped 'em and he went to the sheriff."

"You don't mean it."

"Yes sir. Now, the sheriff thought the feller might try it again. And try again he did, in Forest City. But this time he was caught at it. When that man was brought in, the sheriff made him a deal if he'd say where he was buyin' his whiskey."

"And he named old Joe?"

"He did for a fact."

"Hot dog! I sure am obliged to you. I told Joe I'd come down on him if I got the chance. And I aim to. I didn't think it'd be this soon though."

* * *

Jim Henry walked into the café at Sunshine. Except for Joe and one customer eating a hot dog the café was empty. Joe looked at the constable, but made no comment.

Jim Henry grinned, "Alright Joe, you've done it now. I told you if you stepped outta line I'd come down hard on you. Take off yer apron; lock this place up; I'm takin' you to the county jail and you'll stay there 'til the next term of court."

"Jim Henry Tate! What in hell you talking about?"

"The charge is retailin' liquor. I know you've been at it for years. There weren't no proof though, and I've been willin' to not look at you too hard. But yore luck done run out. I got a warrant to bring you in. I ain't got no choice, but if I did it wouldn't matter. Remember how you screwed around with me t'other day?"

"Aw hell Jim Henry, you ain't really gonna take me to jail are you?"

"Yes I am. Just come on. I got a buggy outside. Let's get going. I want to git back home 'fore dark if I can."

Jim Henry had just begun to turn toward the door when out of the corner of his eye he saw Joe with a raised wooden club that must have been leaning against the wall in easy reach. Realizing what was happening, Jim Henry ducked his head and threw up his left shoulder, causing the shoulder to take the force of the blow, and not his head. Immediately the shoulder went numb and Jim Henry fell heavily onto the edge of a small table. The table collapsed and Jim Henry hit the floor, face down.

The constable knew full well that if he remained on the floor he would be severely beaten, kicked and possibly killed. Fortunately, he also realized that a leg from the table had broken off, skidded in front of him, and was within reach of his right hand. Jim Henry clutched the table leg and tried to determine exactly where Joe was. He looked to his left and saw Joe preparing to kick him. With all the strength he could muster Jim Henry rolled away from the kick and swung the table leg at Joe's shin. As table leg hit leg bone there was a crack followed by a scream and a thud as Joe fell to the floor.

Jim Henry rolled further away from Joe and managed to sit up. He saw that Joe was also sitting, holding his shin and moaning as he rocked from side to side. It seemed certain the fight had gone out of

Joe and he would be no further threat. But, what the hell, the constable thought. He leaned forward and swung the table leg into Joe's side. Joe screamed again and fell over. Jim Henry got to his feet, looked down at Joe, and looked around for the hot dog eater, but the customer was no longer there. Jim Henry walked out to the waiting buggy, took a pair of handcuffs from a bag under the buggy seat, and went back into the café.

"You sure 'nuff done played hell now, old son. Now you're guilty of assault on an officer of the law. I'm a good mind to hit yore sorry ass again. Can you set up? I'm gonna put these cuffs on you—behind yer back. You're gonna be mighty uncomfortable ridin' to the lock up."

Joe just continued to moan. Jim Henry tried to flex his shoulder, into which feeling was slowly returning. "You done beat the shit out of my shoulder. I can't help you up. Stand up Joe! I told you I wanna git back home today. I expect you'll be gitting home in about six months or so—depends on how bad a day the judge is havin' when you're in front of 'im. Stand up!"

As Joe made no effort to rise, Jim Henry stepped outside the café and looked around. Two black men were nearby doing something—he could not determine what—with a mule. He yelled, "Hey! You boys help me out for a minute."

Reluctantly, and with some little muttering, the men tied up the mule and came across to the café. "Come on inside. I've got a feller in here can't seem to stand up."

Inside, the two men helped Joe to his feet, and his hands were cuffed behind his back.

"Now if you'll come outside and help Mr. Joe into the buggy I'd be much obliged."

The still moaning and complaining prisoner was settled into the buggy and Jim Henry climbed aboard.

"I thank you boys, and I'm sure Mr. Joe appreciates yer help as well. Take care with that mule now."

Before Jim Henry could get underway Joe said, "At least lock my place up. They's a key beside the cash box in there behind the bar."

Jim Henry's first inclination was to ignore Joe, but after sitting for a moment he said, "Okay. But if you try to run off you might not live to reach the jail. You understand me?"

"Yeah, yeah, just don't let people rob my place 'fore somebody can git over here."

Jim Henry went into the café, found the key, and locked the door. He climbed onto the buggy, put the key in his shirt pocket, snapped the reins and rode away with one angry bootlegger.

* * *

Jim Henry drove back into Boiling Springs just as darkness was beginning to fall in earnest. He left the buggy and horse at the livery stable and walked the three or four blocks to his home. As he entered the house he called, "I hope you didn't throw supper out to the critters. I could sure use a bite or two."

Joann called from the kitchen where she was stringing beans, "Hey, Law Man. I did save you some food. Guess you've had a busy day."

"Pretty much. Glad ever day's not like this 'un."

"You've been real popular today."

"How's that?"

"Both Forrest Hames and Harry Simmons have been sending folk by all day to see if you were home. You better make a point of seeing them pretty quickly in the morning."

"Well, as Broadus always says, 'They's no rest for the wicked.'"

Jim Henry picked up a kettle of water off the stove, went to the back porch and poured hot water into a wash basin. As he was removing his shirt he said, "I expect I know what they're wantin' and I'm not gonna be able to give them no satisfaction. Things're at a standstill on the murder and on the robbery too. I don't really have no idea what to do. Maybe I ought to just try and beat some information out of a feller or two. After today I'm in the mood for it."

Joann put down her beans and joined Jim Henry on the porch.

"Don't joke about that. I know you don't mean it, but somebody might hear you and take it wrong." Then she gasped, "My heavens! What happened to you? The skin's broken on your shoulder and it's all purplish blue!"

"I made the mistake of turnin' my back on Joe Kenny. I had that warrant for his arrest and I didn't think he'd give me no trouble. You see he did though. Git the alcohol honey, and swab down that shoulder."

As Jim Henry washed his face and hands Joann wiped his shoulder with alcohol. Then she washed his back and he turned to face her. "I'm starved, for food—and for lovin'. What comes first?"

"Jim Henry Tate, since Jimmy went to live with his aunt all you think of is sex. Here, let me go and I'll set you out some supper. Maybe then we'll see about that other thing."

DAY FOUR

At five o'clock Jim Henry woke groggily. Something's wrong, he thought. What's wrong? Then he thought, God, I hurt so bad! Finally, fully awake, he remembered. That son of a bitch Joe, he clubbed me. I hope I cracked his rib. I hope he can't walk, the sorry shit.

After trying, with no success, to get back to sleep, Jim Henry tried to creep out of bed without waking Joann, again with no success. He pulled on his trousers and went into the kitchen. After lighting a fire in the stove, he put on shoes and a shirt, and went two doors east to one of the community wells. There, after waiting for two neighboring housewives to do the same, he pumped a bucket of water.

By the time Jim Henry returned and filled the coffee pot and kettle, Joann was busy kneading dough for biscuits. He snuggled up behind her and put his arms around her waist.

"You really think the way to a man's heart is through his stomach?"

"Well, I know that's one way to your heart; but there seems to be one other way. You want livermush this morning?"

"Of all the things I'd like to have right now, that's high on the list. I think it might be number two."

Jim Henry loved the mixture of pork fat, cornmeal, and cooked, ground pork liver, which was a staple of the mill hill diet. Occasionally sage and/or red pepper would also be mixed in. This mixture was cooked to the consistency of a thick gruel, then placed in loaf pans where it cooled and congealed.

Joann took a butcher-paper wrapped loaf of livermush from the ice box and cut several slices; these were then placed in a hot skillet, which had been well greased with lard. The slices were browned on both sides, and then placed on a plate and set on the stovetop to stay warm. Next the pan in which the livermush slices had been browned was used to make a thick gravy. The biscuits—covered with gravy—and livermush, along with coffee, made a breakfast that came near taking the constable's mind off his aching shoulder.

As the couple ate, Jim Henry planned his day.

"I better git in to see Forrest Hames first thing. I expect he's wantin' me to arrest somebody for shootin' Snag. 'Course I can't do that, but he'll expect it. Then I'll check by to see Harry. He wants me to tell him who's robbin' his store. I can't do that neither. So after I let them both bluster and whine, I think I'll try to find out when Snag was seen last, and if anybody seen Rafer out and about Saturday or Sunday. It had to've been sometime Saturday, or just maybe Sunday, Snag got shot."

Jim Henry sipped his coffee, and sighed. The day ahead was one he would rather avoid.

* * *

Forrest Hames sat in his office and told himself to relax. Things would work out—they always did. But where, he wondered, was Jim Henry Tate? And how would it be possible to hire colored workers without causing a white backlash? Anyway, why did the operatives in cotton mills object to having coloreds working in the same mill? No one objected to having Mose, for example, lay stone for a house that would be built by white carpenters. Indeed, those white carpenters might work on the house side by side with Mose. No one objected to colored men driving wagonloads of cotton to the gin where it would be ginned by white workers. Hames sat and stared out his office window.

It must be, he finally thought, that work in a textile mill was regarded as a somewhat more talented occupation than draying or masonry. Was it? No, he did not think so. After more staring, he thought perhaps—just perhaps—yes, that must be it! Since textile workers were looked down on by some in the white community, they in turn wanted to make their occupation appear better than some others by shutting out blacks.

Reaching this conclusion gave Forrest no comfort. He looked at his calendar and noted he was to meet next Thursday with the county school board to see about getting a colored school established in the village. He looked at the letters in his in-basket. One of the young men in the mill office had approached the owner of a plant in Charlotte looking for a position, and the owner had let Forrest know. Hames chuckled and wondered if he should tell the young man he knew of his shopping around.

Then, "Thunderation!" he said; "I can't sit here and wait for Tate to appear."

With that Forrest stormed out of his office shouting to his secretary that he would be at the company store.

* * *

Harry Simmons was standing in the millinery department of the store. His intention had been to keep an eye on the men's department without Hoyle, Rat Tail or Byron being aware they were under surveillance. But his mind had wandered. First he thought of the milliner—who was, to be sure, a very striking woman. Then he thought of the matched pair of horses he had recently bought from Dr. Lattimore. He had wondered how much money the doctor had. He knew Lattimore held stock in Boiling Springs Mills, and several other textile mills as well. If Lattimore was as rich as rumor had it, he was making money faster than he could spend it.

Now he was thinking that his secretary, Eula, was certainly expecting him to ask that she accompany him to the dinner for store employees his uncle was having Saturday evening. Suddenly he became aware that Forrest Hames was standing before him demanding, "Where is your mind boy? You must be a thousand miles away."

"Oh! Umm. Sorry Uncle Forrest. I was just, uh, thinking about what sort of men's coats we should stock for the winter season. Have to plan those things well ahead you know."

"Well son, you can think about that in your office. When you're on the floor your mind should be on the floor—thinking about what your staff is doing and, I might add, thinking if your staff is too big. Could you get by paying one less salary?"

"I don't think we're overstaffed. But I'll certainly think about it Uncle Forrest. I'll see if maybe we could get by with one or two less people."

Hames threw up his hands. "Boy, you don't seem to understand! This is not an idea I should have to put in your head. You should be thinking all the time about how to reduce cost and increase profits. I don't know Harry, if you're going to make a businessman, or not."

* * *

As Jim Henry entered the company store he saw Forrest Hames practically nose to nose with his nephew, and Harry looked none too happy. He wondered if he should turn around and leave. Would Harry blurt out something about the robberies and pretty well cook his own goose? The decision was taken out of his hands however. Hames noticed Harry's reaction when he saw Jim Henry, and turning, himself saw the constable. He immediately left Harry and closed on Jim Henry.

"Well, it's high time you got here constable. I've been looking for you for more than a day. Let's go upstairs. We can use Harry's office for our conversation."

Walking toward the stairs, Hames addressed Harry.

"You stay down here and think about your staff; the constable and I will need some privacy."

Forrest Hames swept past Harry's secretary without a word and marched into the store manager's office. Following Hames into the office, Jim Henry said, "Good morning Miss Eula; I hope it's okay if we use Harry's office for a few minutes."

"Well, ... uh, I, uh...yes, I suppose it'll be, ... umm, alright. Mr. Simmons isn't here at the moment ... so ... umm, well..."

Jim Henry closed the door as he entered and took a seat in front of the desk—behind which Hames had settled himself.

"So constable, what progress have you made? I hope you are about to arrest someone—someone not living on The Line."

Jim Henry shook his head. "It would be real good if I could do that Mr. Hames. But the truth is I ain't no closer to that point than I was on Tuesday. My day was pretty well used up on other things yesterday."

"Thunderation man! I need to hire some of our coloreds to open bales; you know that's going to be touchy. And you also know 'touchy' is the best I can hope for. If we've had some colored kill a white man—even a worthless scoundrel like Zebulon—well I just don't know what might happen."

"I understand all that Mr. Hames. But I ain't no miracle worker."

"Well, I want miracles if that's what it takes. I tell you what constable; if you haven't satisfied yourself as to who killed Snag by this time next week, I want you to arrest Rafer Jones. He's probably the one anyway."

"Mr. Hames, I don't think I can just up and do that."

"Don't tell me what you can and can't do. I can have the sheriff direct you to arrest Rafer. And I will if you can't arrest somebody else in the time I've given you. That's all! Out you go!"

As Jim Henry was going out by a wide eyed Eula, Hames called, "Just a minute constable. I'm having a dinner party for the store staff at my home this Saturday. I'd be pleased if you and your good wife would attend as well."

It seemed to Jim Henry that the tone of the invitation was the same as the tone with which he had just been dismissed, but he replied,

"That's mighty kind of you Mr. Hames. I'll have to check with Joann though."

"Be there at 6:30 constable!"

* * *

Harry was near the foot of the stairs trying to look as if he was not waiting for his uncle to let him reclaim his office.

The constable walked by without pause and said softly, "I'm going downstairs to hide out in hardware. When your uncle leaves, you come get me and we'll talk."

Downstairs, several farmers were purchasing rope, guano, salt blocks and a variety of items they were unable to produce for themselves. The two clerks had no time for chatting, so Jim Henry approached a couple of men who were standing near the door at the back of the large store building, a door that gave access to the basement from ground level.

"Howdy boys. How're the crops doin' this year?"

Both men chuckled. "Ain't as bad as it might be," one remarked. "The late frost this year was a real bastard. But the rain's been good. Looks like we might make some corn; and cotton seems to be comin' along."

The second man added, "Soon's we pay Forrest Hames the money we owe for seed and fertilizer though, we'll be lucky to have enough to buy the young 'uns some shoes 'fore winter. Hell, if we're real lucky we might even be able to buy a candy cane and an orange or two to give 'em come Christmas." He shook his head, "Makes a man almost want to give up, move into one of them company houses and take up public work." But then he said, "Almost, but not quite. I'm still my own man."

There was nothing Jim Henry could think of to say in response. Instead he asked, "You boys heard about ole Snag I guess?"

Both men nodded. "Yep. Too bad about that, even if Snag was a right bad 'un."

"Well I ain't even close to finding out who shot the ole son.

Either of you boys see Snag recently? I think it might help if I could find out the last time anybody seen him."

One of the men replied, "I don't recall when I seen Snag. Been a long time though. I can't be no help to you Jim Henry."

"I recollect that I saw him at the trade lot last week. Maybe it was about this time last week. That help any?"

"No I'm afraid not. But I'm obliged to you both."

It was only after a further ten or so minutes of unhelpful conversation, followed by another ten or so minutes examining plows, ax handles and nails, that Harry Simmons appeared and motioned for Jim Henry to follow him up to his office.

As the men entered the manager's office, Jim Henry said, "Hello again Miss Eula. This office is seein' lotsa traffic today, ain't it?"

Eula smiled, "It must just be that you're an important man. It seems everybody's wanting to bend your ear. It's always a pleasure to see you, constable."

The two men settled in the chairs in front of the manager's desk. Harry asked, "Have you had any ideas about my little problem Jim Henry?"

"Hell's bells Harry! It's only been a little over a day and I spent yesterday gittin' hell beat outta me and drivin' a man to the jail up yonder in the county seat. Have you been doin' more floor walkin'?"

"Yeah I have, but I ain't seen a thing. I did have a idea, though. I asked Uncle Forrest to invite you and Joann to his party Saturday. Maybe mixin' with the clerks you can get some hint about who's doin' the stealin'."

Jim Henry smiled, "So, that's why I'm suddenly commanded to appear at Hames' shindig? I guess it can't hurt. But I don't expect a lot. You ought not over-expect neither. But here, I've got other problems. When's the last time you saw Snag?"

"Oh, I don't know. Let's see. I think last week—maybe it was Friday—he was in here, in the men's department as I recall."

"Well, that's at least a day or more before I think he was shot. I don't know that that helps even a mite."

"You know, as I remember now, I thought it was funny to see ole Snag looking at men's clothes. I never seen him in any thing but overalls, and they always looked like they was old and wore out. But, I guess he must've bought new clothes sometime."

Jim Henry began to hum and look at the ceiling. After what seemed a long time, but was probably no more than a half minute, Harry made as if to comment. But Jim Henry held up his hand to signal Harry should wait.

After another pause Harry asked, "What're you onto Jim Henry?"

"I ain't sure. I may be onto a idea. It may mean somethin'—and it may not. Anyway, what was you goin' to say?"

"Hmmm, damned if I ain't forgot. It must not've been important."

Jim Henry waited to see if Harry had anything else to say. Then he stood. "Well, okay then. You keep an eye on yer clerks. I've got more fish to fry. See you Saturday at Hames' place, if not before."

The constable left the office. Apparently he did not hear Eula's goodbye.

Outside the store, Jim Henry stopped. He looked up Main Street, then east toward Puzzle Creek; at first he took no notice when Amos passed and said, "Mornin' Jim Henry." But then he yelled after the undertaker, "Wait up Amos!"

Amos stopped and waited as Jim Henry approached. "How are you Jim Henry? Seems like you was miles away just now."

"I was just thinkin' about somethin'. As it turns out though, I'm awful glad you passed by. I need to ask about Snag's buryin'."

"But you was there. What about his buryin'?"

"Well, not exactly the puttin' of him in the ground. What was he wearing?"

Amos looked puzzled. Then he shrugged, and said, "I found some old wool pants in his house, and a shirt that weren't too wore out. Why would you ask?"

"Oh, just somethin' I was wondering about. So the clothes he was buried in were old? Not new?"

"They sure weren't new. They'd seen right much use, I reckon."

The constable slapped Amos on the back. "Thank you Amos. I'll see you around."

As Jim Henry walked slowly away across the square, toward the southeast, Amos shook his head and said, "I reckon you will."

As he walked, Jim Henry's pace quickened and soon he was at the house formerly occupied by Snag Wiley. The house was unlocked, as were all the houses in the village, and Snag's few possessions were still inside. Jim Henry entered the house and sat in one of the chairs at the wobbly, scarred kitchen table. Snag was buried in old wool work pants and a much used shirt. He wondered, did the man have no decent clothes?

The constable rose and walked through the small house. There were no closets. In the bedroom a few worn shirts and a pair of overalls hung from nails driven into the wall. The room itself contained only a bed and a large trunk. Inside the trunk were socks, drawers, some long johns, and in the very bottom a large worn Bible. These large family Bibles usually contained pages on which were listed birth, marriage and death dates for family members. Jim Henry lifted the Bible out, and absently leafed through it searching for those records. Soon he saw a dollar bill that had been slipped between the pages. Continuing to flip through the Bible he saw a five dollar bill, and another one.

"I'll be damned. What is this?" he muttered.

Back at the kitchen table Jim Henry went slowly through the Bible's pages. A total of thirty three dollars had been hidden therein. Several thoughts clamored simultaneously for the constable's attention.

This money would pay for Snag's buryin'.

How did Snag accumulate so much money?

He was up to no good.

I should see Snag's widow gets this money.

This money's stolen.

In a moment of clarity Jim Henry saw that Snag must sure

enough have been connected in some way with the thefts from the company store. He needed to dig a little deeper.

* * *

Back at the company store, Jim Henry went directly to the milliner.

"Hello Rose. How are things with hats?"

"Hello Mr. Tate. As is always the case, things could be better. But we have enough fashion conscious ladies to keep us profitable. Are you looking to buy your wife a hat?"

"No ma'am. I'm just tryin' to find out who killed Snag Wiley. I don't guess you remember seein' Snag? Did you even know who he was?"

"Oh, Mr. Tate! I knew Mr. Wiley—despicable man that he was. Can you imagine? He had the nerve to approach me in a manner which assumed a familiarity that did not, and I might add could not, exist! He was around here far too often."

"Far too often? So Snag was in here a lot?"

"It certainly seemed that way. He seemed to hang about in men's furnishings a great deal."

Jim Henry smiled, "Thank you Rose. I'm not real sure yet, but I think you've been a whole lotta help. It's been a real pleasure talkin' with you."

The constable walked home, went directly through the kitchen, and took a bottle of buttermilk from the ice box. He poured himself a glass, and sat on the back steps sipping his drink. Joann was gathering turnip greens from the garden, unaware that her husband had returned. Shortly however, she saw Jim Henry and came to sit beside him. "Hey, Law Man. How's your morning been?"

"I don't know if it's been a good mornin' or not. But, here's what I know. Snag Wiley had no clothes better'n what you'd put on a scarecrow. Still, he was in the men's department of the company store pretty often. More than that, I found thirty three dollars hid in his old family Bible. Now I'm thinkin' that's got to mean Snag was involved in stealin' from the company store. If that's so, then he had a partner who most likely works in the store."

"So, is that good news or bad news?"

"I guess it's good because the one who shot him might've been the one involved with him in the stealin'. That could mean I'm closer to findin' who killed Snag. But it's also bad 'cause it just means they's one more suspect to throw in with Rafer Jones and some colored man that I don't know. Is that goin' ahead or backin' up?"

"I see what you mean."

"And, I guess I don't have to say, you don't mention what I just said, especially not in yore writin'."

"Jim Henry! How long have we been married? How long have you been constable? You know what you say to me doesn't go any farther. And didn't I check with you before I sent off my column Tuesday? Now, come on in and let me get a bowl. You're gonna crumble some cold cornbread in that butter milk and that's it as far as food goes 'til tonight. I've got too much housework to do to fix you anything hot right now."

* * *

Jim Henry spent the afternoon trying to more closely nail down the time Snag had been shot. Snag had been seen in the village as late as six thirty Saturday evening, give or take a bit. No one could be found who claimed to have seen him later. Also no one could remember, or would admit, seeing Rafer for eight or nine days, anywhere except sitting in his yard or on his porch.

Some time before six the constable decided any more time spent asking folk when they last saw Snag or Rafer would simply be time wasted. He decided to visit the company store, touch base with Harry, and go home for his supper.

Once again Jim Henry found Harry on the store floor. When Harry saw the constable, he pointed up toward his office and Jim Henry went up ahead of him. Eula was busily doing something in the depths of her oversized purse and if she was surprised seeing Jim Henry for a third time, she hid her surprise well.

"Hi constable, Harry's not here. Oh! I see. He's just behind you."

"Looks like you're about to close up shop Miss Eula."

As Harry entered his office he said, "You can go on Eula. There'll be no more need for you today." And to Jim Henry he said, "Didn't expect to see you again so soon. You must have made some progress."

The men entered the manager's office, closed the door, and Jim Henry said, "I believe I have. I got to thinking about Snag in the men's department. That seemed damn strange, 'cause I didn't think he had any new clothes. So I went to his house, and sure enough, any clothes in that place would near 'bout embarrass a colored beggar. But here's what's really important. I found thirty three dollars hid in his Bible. All this together makes it look like Snag was in on yore thefts."

Harry smiled and slowly replied, "Well, I'll be dipped! That sounds right Jim Henry." But his smile quickly faded. "But dammit, that pretty much says one of my menswear clerks is guilty."

"That's how I feel about it. And, I checked with Rose—she has a clear view of men's wear—and she says Snag was in that department right regular. But now which of the clerks could it be? I'd trust any one of 'em."

"I hate to think it's any of 'em. But I don't hardly see how it's not."

"Well, which one would it be?"

"Hoyle's considered to be a pillar of the community by ever body. He come here about the time the mill was bein' built. He was on the buildin' committee for the church and he's a Pythian and a Red Man." Harry paused, shrugged his shoulders, and then continued. "But, his wife has been sickly for a long time. He might be needin' money pretty bad."

Jim Henry shook his head. "Harry, I believe I'd rule Hoyle out anyway."

"Okay. Then there's Rat Tail. There's never been anything against him—except he don't stand up to his witchy wife. I guess she's never satisfied with her station and Rat Tail might've tried to bring in a little extra money on the side. But then why would he be in cahoots with Snag? Why would any one of 'em, for that matter?"

"Yeah. There's a problem. None of yer clerks run with Snag. How'd Snag get into it?"

"I couldn't figure."

"While we're at it, how about Byron?"

"Well, Byron's the youngest, and young folks sometimes go wild. He might've got to runnin' with Snag and his crowd. In fact, he's more likely to have hooked up with Snag than the others. But he's a good man. His family's good people. It's just hard to see Byron stealin' from the store."

Jim Henry sat and stared at the floor for a minute or so. "Could I be wrong? Could Snag have come up with that money some honest way—or some other dishonest way? I wonder." After a bit he said, "No. Damn it Harry, it just fits together too good. Snag had to be involved with stealin' from the store. And somebody clerkin' for you was in it too."

"I think you're right. And I think it's one in menswear—much as I wish it weren't."

The men sat in silence for a while. Then Jim Henry said, "Well my supper's callin' me. You keep yer eyes open and I'll do what I can. Maybe yore bright idea will pan out and I'll learn somethin' at Hames' place Saturday."

Harry walked the constable to the head of the stairs and stood staring into space as he left.

* * *

Jim Henry was in high spirits as he sat down to his supper. Joann had cooked pinto beans, fried potatoes, baked cornbread and made up a fresh bowl of slaw. As he sliced raw onion over the pinto beans the constable sighed with satisfaction. When Joann joined him at the table, Jim Henry said, "Hope you've got a pretty dress ready for Saturday night."

"Why's that?"

"Well, I forgot to tell you before, but we're in high society. I reckon around here the constable is way up yonder on the social scale."

"What are you talking about?"

"We're going to a wingding at Hames' house."

"Well then! I guess we'll eat better Saturday than we're eating today."

"Oh I doubt that. I couldn't ask for better myself. 'Course Hames might have stew beef. We ain't had that in a while."

Joann ate for a few moments and then asked, "How come we're invited? I don't think I've been in Mr. Hames' house but once. That was with a church group he had in for a prayer meeting."

Jim Henry paused as he was buttering a slice of cornbread and said, "Oh, Harry asked his uncle to invite us. Hames is havin' the store clerks in and Harry thinks I might learn somethin' mixin' with 'em. I don't hold out much hope, but you never know."

The couple continued to eat in silence for a while. Then Jim Henry asked, "Any more of them potatoes?"

"Yes, I'll get you some."

He smiled, "How about that 'other thing' we had last night? Any more of that, do you reckon?"

DAY FIVE

As it turned out, Jim Henry's day began much earlier Friday than he would have liked. He awoke in the dark—certain he had heard a noise that was out of place. It was raining steadily, with an occasional roll of thunder. Perhaps, he thought, it was thunder that had wakened him. But as he rolled over and settled again into his pillow he heard a soft tapping. Was it coming from the kitchen? He decided he'd best check. Perhaps an animal of some sort had managed to get into the house. He rose from the bed as quietly as he could and tiptoed into the kitchen. Then he heard the tapping once again; it was now clear the noise was coming from the back porch. Opening the kitchen door, he looked out. But he could see nothing amiss.

A voice whispered, "Mr. Jim Henry? Mr. Jim Henry, it's Mose. I hope you don't have yore pistol Mr. Jim Henry. Nothin' to be 'fraid about Cap'n."

The constable was suddenly wide awake and, looking in the direction of Mose's voice, he was barely able to make out the black man standing just off the back porch and to the left of the steps.

"Come on up on the porch Mose. Git outta the rain. What in the name of God are you about?"

"I need to speak with you a minute Cap'n, and I don't want nobody knowin' I been here or been talkin' to you. I'm fixin' to tell you somethin' you likely wanna know. I hope Jesus forgive me if I'm doin' wrong."

Mose came up and stood just off the top step, barely out of the rain. Jim Henry leaned against the large ice box that sat on the porch.

"Well, here I am Mose. It's damned early but it must be mighty important for you to walk over here from The Line in this pourin' rain. What is it you got to say?"

Mose removed his hat and held it to his chest with both hands. "You know LuElla, Marvin's girl?"

"Of course I know her Mose. She helps her aunt sometimes with the cookin' and cleanin' at Mr. Hames' house. I hear she's a fine girl."

"She is that, Mr. Jim Henry. But she done been beat without mercy. She been beat on with some sorta leather strap it look like. She walkin' like her legs and back pretty bad wore out. And she got a mighty bad cut on her face."

"Well hell Mose, I'll find the bastard who did that! But is that what you don't want folks knowin' you told me? I don't understand."

"I just sho' don't want nobody knowin' I told you 'bout this. That's all."

"Come on Mose. I'll arrest whoever beat her like that. If he's white it don't make a damn bit of difference. Her getting' beat on is just plain wrong."

"I ain't sayin'no white man beat her, Mr. Jim Henry. You think on that, Cap'n. That's all I have to say, and I'll claim I didn't say it. Good mornin' now, Mr. Jim Henry. I'm right sorry I had to wake you."

"Wait Mose! You must know more than you're tellin' me. Why is it important that I know LuElla was beat on?"

"No, I done told you all I know Cap'n. And I ain't sayin' no more."

Mose disappeared into the early morning blackness as lightening flashed and thunder cracked with an explosive boom.

Jim Henry stood and puzzled. What in hell was that all about? After a bit, certain he could not get back into bed without waking Joann, he went into the front room of the house and sat in his favorite rocker. But he couldn't get comfortable in the rocker, so after a while, he moved out onto the front porch where he managed to curl up, more or less horizontally, in the swing.

As the first hint of dawn was creeping over the horizon, Jim Henry was startled awake when Joann asked, "What are you doing out here in your drawers Jim Henry?"

The constable struggled into an upright position. His sore shoulder ached and his legs were cramped. "Ouch! Oh my God!" he groaned.

"Well?"

"I must've dropped off."

"I see that. But why are you not in bed?"

The constable stretched and yawned. "In a way, I don't know. But I had a visitor early on and I didn't think I could git back in bed without wakin' you."

"Well get in the house right now. People are gonna be walking by going to work just any time now."

Jim Henry went in and put on trousers, an undershirt and his gardening shoes. He went to the privy at the back of their lot. Then he went for water while Joann started a fire in the kitchen stove. Leaving his muddy shoes on the kitchen porch, he took the water in and put a kettle on to heat. When the water was hot, he took some of it back out to the porch where he shaved, brushed his teeth and combed his hair. When he went back into the kitchen, his morning coffee was sitting on the table.

"Well Law Man, while you drink your coffee, tell me about this night visitor. You sure it wasn't a dream?"

Looking at Joann over the cup he was holding, Jim Henry said, "Not a dream. It was Mose. He showed up some time ago—I didn't make a light to see the time. He said he'd come to tell me somethin' I wanted to know. Maybe he did, but he might's well been speakin' in tongues."

"What exactly did he say?"

"He said somebody's beat LuElla badly. You know her; she's one of Marvin's girls. And that's all of it." The constable sighed. "What do you reckon that's all about?"

After a moment Joann replied, "I don't know."

"Well, it must be important. Them biscuits done?"

"No they're not. You'll just have to wait a while more. You think about Mose and what he said."

After several sips of coffee, Jim Henry shrugged. "I guess I'll have to talk with LuElla and see if I can figure out what Mose was up to. 'Course if I let on that I know all about her getting whipped, she'll wonder how I found out, and one thing will lead to another, and another, and then, maybe, to Mose."

"If you can't say you know about her being whipped, what reason will you have to visit LuElla?"

"None I can think of."

Joann took her biscuits from the oven and dumped them into a basket lined with a clean dish towel. Jim Henry took one immediately, and because it was piping hot he quickly dropped it on his plate. As he sliced the biscuit open and put a large pat of butter inside he said, "LuElla'll probably be at Hames' dinner tomorrow; maybe I can corner her there." He took a bite of biscuit, chewed and added, "Before that maybe I'll walk through The Line and see what I can see. But first, I've still got Joe Kenny's keys. I guess I ought to take them to his wife. I expect she has another set, but I don't have any need for 'em."

* * *

As he would pass not too far from Rafer Jones' house on his way to the livery stable, Jim Henry decided to stop by and see how Jones was recuperating. He also thought it a good idea to make sure his suspect had not left town.

At the Jones home, Rafer was not to be seen. Jim Henry scraped mud from his boots on the edge of the porch, stepped to the door and knocked. A voice from inside yelled, "Who is it?"

"It's Jim Henry; can you git about yet Rafer?"

Rafer came to the door, walking slowly but without obvious signs of pain. "I'm doin' some better. I hope to go back to work next week. Why're you here again? I told you all I can tell you—mainly that I didn't do it!"

"I know you say that. And maybe you didn't. But I gotta find out who did do it. Accordin' to some of the loafers at The State Line, Snag fought with folks other than you."

"Yeah, he did."

"You run with ole Snag for quite a time, so you know his buddies, and I bet you know them folks he beat up. Since you tell me you didn't kill 'im, who in that State Line crowd do you think might have?"

"Ah, God Jim Henry, I don't think nobody in that crowd killed him. I've thought about it, and since Snag was messin' with some colored gal I expect it was somebody from The Line. Why ain't you over there lookin'?"

"Wouldn't you know, I'll be on The Line after a while. But they's no evidence any of our coloreds killed Snag."

"They's no evidence I done it!"

"And that's why you're still home in the bosom of yore family, and not in the county lockup. Let's see if you can help yoreself stay outta that county jail. Is they anything you didn't tell me last time I was here? Anything else Snag said, or anything one of his buddies said?"

"No, no and no! I told you before, they's nothing else I know. I know this though, I didn't kill Snag!"

Jim Henry just looked at Rafer and waited for him to add something. When he did not he said, "Okay then Rafer. Good to see you're getting back to yer hell-raisin' self. Don't be surprised when you see me again."

* * *

Jim Henry tied his horse to a bush beside the trade lot mule pen. He was somewhat surprised to see that the café was apparently doing a brisk—better than average—business. Remembering the mistake he'd made on his last visit, the constable entered the café slowly so that his eyes could adjust to the dim light. Just inside the door he moved to the left and stopped with his back to the wall. There were more than a dozen men sitting and standing around, and Joe's wife Ruby Charles was behind the counter.

Ruby Charles was a buxom, red haired woman in her early thirties. And her speech and actions were looked on by the village women as somewhat too free. No doubt some, well, perhaps all, of the café's customers were there in hopes they could entertain her in Joe's absence.

When Ruby Charles saw Jim Henry she called out, "You can go straight to hell Constable Tate!"

"Good morning to you too, Ruby Charles. Looks like business has picked up with Joe gone."

"Don't try to be funny with me. Joe was arrested on the word of some black skunks, weren't he? And you had no call to beat on Joe like you did."

"That's not the way of it Ruby Charles, and I think you know it. I wouldn't have laid a hand on Joe if he hadn't tried to knock my head off. He coulda served a couple weeks for sellin' liquor and been through with it. But now he'll see six months on the road, 'less I'm mighty wrong."

"Like I said before, you go to hell!"

The constable just threw the keys to Ruby Charles, left the café and walked to a group of men gathered at the trade lot.

Jim Henry had expected hostility in the café. He anticipated none from the men near the mule pen, and there was none, none directed at him, that is. But there was hostility to spare. Immediately he joined the group, one of the men demanded, "Is it true some colored killed ole Snag?"

"Where'd you git that idea?"

Several men spoke at once.

"It's what ever body's sayin'."

"We hear Snag was screwin' a colored gal. Figures somebody on The Line took it on to stop that. Killin' Snag shore stopped it."

"Maybe we oughta hang one or two a them. That'd teach 'em to leave white men alone!"

Jim Henry held up his hand and slowly the noise subsided.

"Now boys, they's absolutely nothin' to even hint that Snag's killer's from The Line. Nothin' but yore imagination. It'll help me find who did kill 'em if I don't have to spend time trying to keep you boys from doin' something stupid and breakin' the law. Let's don't hear no more talk of this lynchin' business!"

"Well if it weren't one of them from The Line, who done it?"

"Surely you boys know it coulda been Rafer Jones. But it coulda not been. They's not a speck of evidence against Rafe either. I'm workin' on it boys. Just give me a little time. I can guarantee they'll be an arrest by Thursday. How's that? Now just settle."

This was followed by a general muttering. Of course, Jim Henry thought, it damn well may be Rafe that gets arrested and you won't like that!

One of the men couldn't let it rest, "If you don't put one of 'em in jail, we'll settle some black hide Jim Henry," he said.

Jim Henry decided there was not really anything he could do to calm things at this point. His best move was to just leave. But first he said, "Don't let me have to throw some of you boys in jail. Just quit this rilin' yoreselves up over somethin' that more'n likely ain't a fact."

Jim Henry walked to his horse, untied the reins and mounted; he was all too conscious of the continuing angry talk among the men. And it was all too clear he'd best be getting ready for trouble.

* * *

The constable had ridden slowly back to the village. As he rode he had brooded. Folks might work themselves into a state where something like a lynching was a real possibility. That's if he couldn't find the killer. And, the killer might actually be black. What then? How would he go about keeping order?

Scott Blanton sat outside the livery stable reading last week's issue of the *Three Mills Gazette*. The *Gazette* was in fact nothing more than a template that was used by numerous small newspapers. Mostly it reported national news. However, each of its four pages did contain a few spots for local items. Local items were local to the county at large for the most part. Only the larger towns and villages received anything like regular coverage. Because of Joann's reporting, Boiling Springs was fortunate to get a little press more frequently than most.

Jim Henry hailed Blanton, who got up to take the constable's horse.

"Howdy Scott. Looks like we might get another rain before the day's over."

"Might be. If so, looks like we'll be swimmin' in mud."

Jim Henry dismounted. "Scott, I'm gonna need some help in the next few days, unless I miss my bet. Wonder if I could call on you?"

Blanton looked taken aback. "What sorta help, Jim Henry?"

"Well, they's a buncha hot heads got the idea somebody on The Line killed Snag. If they get worked up enough they're gonna go out yonder and try to hurt some of our coloreds. I can't stand by and let that happen. But I need a couple men to stand with me."

"I, .. I, .. I'm not too sure what you'd want me to do Jim Henry."

Jim Henry stood silent for rather a long time while Scott shuffled and looked uncomfortable.

"I think maybe you are sure Scott. Maybe that's why you're slow to say you'll help out. It might come to the point where I'll have to bust somebody's head. May have to shoot somebody if things get bad enough. Whoever I have with me, I'll expect them to do the same—if they's a need."

"Well, ... well, ... maybe you're right about me. I can't see shootin' a white man to shelter a black 'un. Just can't see it."

"Okay Scott. Rather you tell me now, than me git in a bind and have you not back me."

"Hope they's no hard feelings Jim Henry. You know I back you generally, but, well, ... we ain't talkin' general."

"Don't give it another thought Scott." Jim Henry turned to go, then turned back. "But I would be grateful if you'd stay home if some wild bunch starts toward The Line tryin' to get a crowd to go with 'em. If you won't help me, at least don't get crosswise of me."

"Oh come on Jim Henry, you know I wouldn't get in no rag tag crowd like that."

After a pause that Scott found—and Jim Henry intended—embarrassing, the constable said, "Uh huh."

* * *

Jim Henry walked from the livery stable to the cotton gin east of the square, just north of the textile plant. He still needed to line up the support he was afraid he would soon need. When he arrived at the gin, Broadus White was busy dickering over a wagon load of cotton—four bales. There was a house directly opposite the gin, and in the yard of the house was a small magnolia tree. The constable walked over and sat in the shade of the tree, with his back against the trunk, waiting to see the cotton buyer finish his transaction. The deal was not struck quickly and Jim Henry soon stood up as he felt the seat of his pants becoming damp. The grass under the tree had not dried completely since the night's rain.

Finally Broadus was free and Jim Henry went quickly to catch him before he became involved in another purchase.

"Broadus, I need to talk to you. You got a minute?"

"Hey, Jim Henry. Looks like I got more than a minute; might have two or three. What's on your mind?"

"Nothing good. They's startin' to be talk that one of our coloreds shot Snag Wiley. They's no evidence of that, but it don't matter none when that kinda talk starts. I'm thinkin' I'm gonna have some work to do soon and I'm lookin' for some help."

"You mean you're wantin' to deputize me?"

"Don't really think I got the authority to deputize anybody. Probably the sheriff has to do that. But I reckon I am askin' if you'd act as a deputy."

"Gonna be touchy if we have to break somebody's head—or worse. Protectin' coloreds against whites don't make a man popular in this county."

"You say if 'we' have to break a head. That mean you'll help me out?"

"Well hell yes, Jim Henry. Did you doubt it? Besides if worse comes to worst, not that many people like me anyway. At least half the farmers think I might be in league with the devil. 'Course I just drive a hard bargain." He chuckled, "The mill workers think I spy, or worse, for Forrest Hames. And, maybe, in a way, I do a little bit."

"I'm sure grateful. I hope it won't be just me and you if it comes to it. I'm gonna try to line up one more. But—come time—plan to load yer shotgun with bird shot. That ought not kill nobody, but it'll tear up a body's hide, if things get too iffy. I'm gonna start carrying my revolver too. A little fear could be a good thing."

"You just call on me, Jim Henry. We can't have white trash stirrin' things up; and we sure as hell ain't gonna have no lynchin' like they did in Forest City."

Jim Henry reached to shake his friend's hand, "Again, I'm grateful Broadus. I surely hope I don't have to call on you. But I'm gonna go on now and try to line up one more. Three with weapons should cool most hot heads. 'Course I don't know who to try next."

"Try Zeno. Near 'bout all the mill operatives is just one payday away from bein' hungry, and if they don't have a mill house they don't have no house a-tall. It's mill hands we'll have to deal with. Just seein' the super might do as much good as bird shot."

Jim Henry grinned, "That's a good idea. And Broadus, again, I'm obliged to you."

* * *

When he arrived at Zeno Harris' office, Jim Henry was told that the super was in the mill, but expected back shortly. So he sat waiting and idly scanning the *Southern Textile Bulletin*. He noted that under the listing of Southern Textile Stocks the Boiling Springs Mills showed $190 bid and $200 asked. He laid the magazine down and wondered how anybody managed to set aside enough money to buy even one share. It was rumored, he recalled, that Forrest Hames owned twenty five hundred shares.

The outer office in which he waited was rather warm and Jim Henry had almost dozed off when the plant superintendent came in and said, “What did I do constable? And how did you find out about it?”

Jim Henry was embarrassed that Zeno had startled him out of a light doze, but he replied, “I’m sure you’ve done somethin’ I ought to know about, but this time I’m here hat in hand. I’m askin’ for help.”

“Well, come on in and talk to me about it.”

The men entered Harris’ office and Jim Henry laid out the reason he feared trouble in the black section. He explained, moreover, that he thought Zeno’s presence at any confrontation would take the wind out of most rabble rouser’s sails.

“Jim Henry, you just call on me if any trouble starts and I’ll get there as fast as I can. I know Mr. Hames wants no trouble with our coloreds and I don’t want any trouble either. But do you think there’s any chance somebody on The Line actually did kill Snag?”

“I don’t think it’ll turn out that way. But much as I hate to say it, they is a chance.”

“If it turns out Snag was killed by a colored you may have to bring in a bunch of law from the county seat to keep things from boiling over. Let’s hope it was a white man shot Mr. Zebulon Wiley. It’ll be better for everybody. But look here, you have no idea who might have done it?”

“Not right now. As I see it, they’s three different possibilities. I don’t know enough now to say which is most likely, though. It would be simple I guess to just arrest Rafer Jones. But I’m thinkin’ it’s less likely he did it than that he didn’t.”

Zeno rose and Jim Henry knew he was being dismissed. “I’m glad my job’s simpler than yours Jim Henry.”

“I’m obliged to you Zeno. Hope I don’t have to call on you.”

The constable was out the office door when he turned back, “In case something does happen—I’m going with my revolver. Broadus’ll be there too and he'll have a shotgun loaded with bird shot. Maybe it won't be that we have to hurt somebody serious."

* * *

It was a bit early for his noonday meal, but since his house was between the mill office and the colored section, Jim Henry decided to stop in and eat something. Maybe, he thought, he might put his feet up for a while as well.

When he arrived home, Jim Henry found his wife absent. There was no sign she had started cooking anything. It looked like another cornbread and buttermilk day. Or perhaps he'd just have some cheese and bread; and maybe, he thought, there might be a boiled egg or two in the ice box. But deciding he would wait a while for Joann, he went into the bedroom, kicked off his boots and stretched out on the bed. Quickly he was sound asleep.

A slamming screen door startled Jim Henry awake. "Joann, that you?"

"Sure is; you expecting some other woman?"

Joann walked into the bedroom.

"What are you doing sleeping the day away?"

Jim Henry stretched and scratched his head, but he made no move to get out of bed.

"I come home lookin' for food and didn't find any. So I tried to think of some place I might find some lovin'. Couldn't think of any place, so I come in here and dropped off."

"You can forget sex. I might find you some food, but it's gonna be cold again today. I've been at the church. The Women's Missionary Union is busy planning the big revival that's coming up. I designed some leaflets that we'll distribute, and we talked about who would house the visiting preacher, who would feed him what meals and such."

"Oh God! We ain't gonna have a preacher here, are we?"

"We just might. With Jimmy over in Lawndale we do have an empty bedroom. Not many people in the village have a spare room—

and them that do usually rent it out. But I said we wouldn't do more than one night."

Jim Henry grimaced.

"Oh come on! He'll be asleep most of the time he's here. So while you might have to behave like a Christian, it'll just be for one supper, and one breakfast. You can manage that."

"Yes ma'am, whatever you say. What about that food?"

"There's cheese and crackers, and we've got some tinned meat. That'll have to do. But I bought a tin of salmon the other day. I'll make salmon patties tonight with potatoes, green beans and hot cornbread. We'll have a treat."

* * *

As the constable walked toward the black section he thought about Mose's early morning visit. Why was it so important that he know LuElla had been beaten? He guessed he'd damn well better find out.

When Jim Henry reached the little café on The Line there were several men still inside eating. Even with all the windows and the door open, it was unpleasantly warm inside the café and June was sitting outside fanning himself.

"Afternoon June. Mind if I set with you a while?"

"No sir Cap'n. You grab one them chairs from inside and settle out here with me. They ain't a breatha air though."

The men sat in companionable silence and watched as people came and went along The Line. Men trickled out of the café as they finished eating. Someone called June from inside and he went to attend to business.

When he came back, Jim Henry said, "June, I ain't gittin' nowhere with Snag's killin'. I surely need somebody that knows somethin' to let me know somethin'. That somebody you?"

June just shook his head and continued to fan himself.

"Things have changed since I talked to you on Monday. In spite of what you, and other folks, say, I know as well as I can know anything that Snag was pokin' one of the women on The Line. Surely if white people know that, colored people's figured it out."

"Can't say about what you know and what you don't Cap'n, but I don't believe it. Mr. Snag was a mean 'un—especially with colored folks. Why would any of our women folks got in bed with him?"

"I can't say. But people do funny things for funny reasons, you know that."

As the men sat in silence, the train came rumbling slowly by, on its way to the junction with the Seaboard Airline.

When it was quiet again June sighed and said, "If some colored woman been messin' with Mr. Snag, her husband would know. And if he know, she might not live through his knowin'."

Jim Henry was afraid to speak, afraid his excitement would show in his voice. He merely nodded and maintained his best poker face. He understood what Mose had told him, and why he'd told him!

Shortly June said, "You set here long as you want, Mr. Jim Henry. I got to git inside, clean up and begin to think about the crowd what stop by after they finish work."

"Oh, I guess I'd best go along. Maybe I can find somebody on The Line who's more talkative than you, June."

Jim Henry now had a clear objective. He needed to casually meet up with LuElla. He could then begin by noticing that she was hurt. From there he could ask how it happened. That opening might or might not lead somewhere. But it now seemed clear that her father had beaten her, and he had done so because she'd been meeting Snag. Somehow the constable needed to learn more about LuElla and Snag, maybe where they had met, and exactly when her carrying on with Snag had been discovered. If her beating had occurred since Monday, it was likely her father had not known about her meeting up with Snag before Monday. In that case he likely was not the murderer, and maybe, just maybe the entire black community could reasonably be eliminated from suspicion. Jim Henry began to hum as he walked up The Line.

For an hour the constable strolled slowly about the black section. He stopped and talked with everyone he met—everyone who would talk with him. But he saw no sign of LuElla and he could find no reason to ask where she might be. Deciding it would be cooler to walk back to the village square along the river bank, he took the path connecting The Line and the river. As he walked down the path, he again began to wonder exactly where Snag could have been killed.

On reaching the river Jim Henry stopped, and sat on a large rock. While I'm here, he thought, I may as well look carefully along the river one more time. So instead of heading directly for the center of the village, he turned to his right and began moving slowly toward the mouth of Corn Mill Creek.

Walking up river he saw nothing of interest, and soon arrived at the creek mouth. Standing by the creek, Jim Henry realized he had overlooked something. He had not considered that Snag might have been shot along the creek bank. But surely the creek was too shallow. If Snag's body had fallen into the creek, the shallow water would not have allowed it to then float into the river. Or would it?

There was a dim, seldom used, path running along the creek toward the grist mill. With a shrug, and convinced he would find nothing of interest, Jim Henry began to follow the faint path. Almost immediately he found something very interesting.

About twenty yards up the creek, an even fainter path intersected the trail at a right angle. Jim Henry followed this path behind a short knoll. There he found that weeds had been flattened over an area of about eight feet by six feet. There were no deer and no bear in the area—the animals using this hideaway were doubtless human. The constable chuckled. He recalled Elvy's comment about sowing human seed. This was, he thought, most likely where Snag had met LuElla. But was that knowledge of any real help? He moved back to the creek bank and studied the area. There was no noticeable disturbance, but then there had been significant rain since Monday. Still, the creek at that point was less than a foot in depth. If Snag had been shot at this spot and fallen into the creek, surely his body would never have floated into the river.

Slowly Jim Henry walked up the creek until the grist mill was in sight. He then retraced his steps, walked back to the river and followed it south until he arrived at the park containing the bandstand. Here he sat on the steps of the bandstand and wondered if he could arrange to talk with LuElla at Hames' dinner, without giving away the fact that Mose had told him about her beating. He sat quietly for a while thinking of tomorrow night's dinner. He needed to enlist Hames' help to approach LuElla.

* * *

When Jim Henry entered Forrest Hames' office, he was told Hames had gone across to the cotton gin. The constable decided to wait, for he feared if he left to catch Hames at the gin, they might miss each other and he would just have to come right back to Hames' office.

In about ten minutes Hames came bustling in and saw Jim Henry waiting. "You have some information for me constable?"

"No sir Mr. Hames, I don't. But I need to speak with you."

"Well come on back, and make it fast. I don't have a lot of time."

Jim Henry followed Hames, took a seat, and explained how he planned to approach LuElla.

Forrest Hames was not a happy man. Here was the local constable, obviously in possession of information he would not share. And he was asking Hames to take actions whose purpose he likewise would not share. He rubbed his face and said, "So you know that my maid's niece has been beaten, but you won't tell me who did it. You won't tell me how you know. And you tell me you can't even let LuElla know that you've already learned of her beating."

"That's right Mr. Hames. All I can say is I'm askin' you to help me, and yore help might shed light on Snag's murder."

"Might? Well thunderation constable! That's not satisfactory at all!"

Jim Henry leaned forward with his elbows on his knees; while staring Hames in the eye he said, "Mr. Hames, you've already give me a deadline for findin' who killed Snag. If I don't meet that deadline you're gonna force me to arrest Rafer Jones—or try to. Don't tie my hands any more. Just help me out. You have to do mighty little. Just notice that LuElla's walkin' funny and has a cut on her face. Ask her what happened. She won't tell you. So then you give me the high sign and I tell her you want me to see about what happened to her."

"How's that going to help?"

Jim Henry sat back. "I can't tell you; and it might not help. But it's the best road I can go down right now. 'Course if you won't help, I'll just let that be a dead end and figure somethin' else."

Hames fiddled with the papers on his desk. He looked out the window, then at Jim Henry. "All right! All right! LuElla will indeed be helping her aunt with tomorrow night's meal. And I'll make a point of noticing her condition and do as you say. Am I ever gonna know what this is all about?"

"I hope not. You won't hear it from me."

"Well thunderation! Get out of here constable! And you'd better have this mess wrapped up come Thursday."

* * *

After their meal Jim Henry and Joann sat on the front porch, speaking to neighbors who walked by or called from their own porch. They hoped to catch an evening breeze.

Joann sighed, "I miss Jimmy. We haven't seen him in more than a month. Let's go visit."

"I'm sorry honey. I just can't go right now. This murder thing's comin' along." He chuckled. "In a way I ain't no nearer determinin' who killed Snag. I do think though I'm gonna learn more about whether the killer's from The Line."

"But do you really have to stay here this weekend?"

"I wish I didn't; but I'm afraid I do. They's a buncha yahoos stirred up 'cause they think one of our coloreds killed Snag. Startin' noon tomorrow, when ever body's off work, things might get hot. I'm gonna start wearin' my revolver in the mornin'."

"Oh my Lord! Surely not!"

"Well, we'll hope I'm wrong. But I'm afraid I really need to be here. I think things are on a simmer and might start to boil."

DAY SIX

Jim Henry normally slept soundly, but in the early morning he awoke. Soon he heard the town clock strike three. The striking of the clock was such a familiar part of village life that often, even during the daylight hours, it could strike without anyone being fully aware of it.

The constable rose, went outside and relieved himself on a hedge that grew between the house and Joann's kitchen garden. He realized he was fully awake, so he sat on the back porch steps and tried to put together all the things he knew about Snag's murder, the theft from the company store, LuElla's involvement with Snag, and Snag's beating of Rafer Jones.

I don't know a thing, he thought. I'm like a water bug skimmin' over the surface of a pond, with no idea what's really goin' on below that smooth, peaceful surface. I *may* know some things, but I don't know what they mean. I can't see below the surface.

The big clock struck four and Jim Henry remained sitting. He had thought and thought about how the things he knew might tie together. Of course it might be that nothing tied to anything else. Maybe there was no big picture. He couldn't really believe that. Certainly Snag's carryin' on with LuElla had a tie to Rafer. He hoped that carryin' on didn't have a tie to Snag's murder. Maybe the theft and the murder could be connected? If so, how? The constable rose and slipped back into bed. He really hoped Joann would wake, for he wanted the comfort of her warm body. But she slept on and he tossed and turned. Sleep eluded him, and he welcomed the beginning of dawn about five thirty.

As Jim Henry was lighting a fire in the kitchen stove, Joann came in behind him and put her arms around him. "I don't think you slept much Law Man."

"No I didn't." He sighed, "My job's pretty soft most of the time. I can just walk around and let people see they's some law in the lower part of the county. Today won't be like that though. And it looks like I'm not gonna be at my best."

"You'll be fine. How about some pancakes?"

"With sausage?"

"Sure, why not? We'll have a big breakfast and just snack along 'til Mr. Hames' big dinner tonight."

"Now you're talkin'. Heat up some of that molasses too. I love molasses over pancakes—if they's no honey."

After breakfast Jim Henry took his revolver from the cedar chest at the foot of the bed and strapped it on. Joann watched from the kitchen.

"I don't like it when you wear that thing."

"I wish it was so I didn't have to wear it. But maybe just seein' me wearin' it will cool some hot heads."

* * *

The village square was filled with the buggies, wagons and horses of farmers from the surrounding country. For the farm families, Saturday was shopping day. And even though they came to buy sugar, salt, flour and other necessities, their trip into the village was also for entertainment. Women could stroll through the company store and admire the ready-to-wear dresses, blouses and hats that few, if any, of them could afford. Children could chase each other around the cotton gin and the mill warehouses, and if they were lucky, they might be treated to a dish of ice cream at the ice cream parlor. Men sat in the shade, smoked, and discussed crops, weather and politics; those with a bit of money might even treat themselves to a haircut and/or shave at the barber shop. It was to the barber shop that Jim Henry went first, for he knew it was in this male retreat that talk was the most free, and sometimes—unfortunately—the most heated.

As the constable entered, there was a pause in the conversation. After a moment the barber said, "Mornin' Jim Henry. You look like you could use a trim."

"I reckon Joann would feel right hurt if I didn't let her cut my hair. I'm just wanderin' around this morning. How's ever thing with you men today?"

There was no immediate response. Finally an older man replied, "I expect we're all tolerable. I notice you're carryin' yore gun today. Is they somethin' brewin'?"

"Oh, I don't know. I guess I just thought maybe the law ought to look like the law ever now and then. The sheriff sort of expects me to act like a constable some of the time."

"Shit, Jim Henry, we all know what's bein' said about ole Snag's killin'. They say Snag was mountin' a black woman up yonder on The Line pretty regular; and folks think some of her male kin took exception to that and shot Snag. Is that the way of it?"

"I can't say that it is. Fact is, they's no evidence at all that Snag's killer was one of our coloreds. For what it's worth, I'm pretty well convinced I'll find the one that killed him's not from The Line a-tall."

A large man in the barber chair spoke up. "You think what you want Jim Henry, and I'll think what I want, and I think you're wrong. Them coloreds ain't like us. Their passions just run hotter. I guess that's why Snag had hisself that black woman; she probably give him somethin' he couldn't git from white women. Look at how them colored men fight and cut each other up nearly ever weekend. They're just more animal than not."

"That's right," the barber chimed in. "I figure that them

coloreds, way back, around the time of Adam and Eve, come from the union of people with apes."

There was a murmur of approval from several of the shop patrons.

"Come on boys," Jim Henry laughed. "You know you can't breed a cow with a horse, or a cat with a dog, how in hell could a person breed with an ape?"

"Well it might not be possible today, but in Bible times lots of things happened we don't see today. You know they was the sun standin' still, and Methuselah livin' nine hundred years or somethin' like that."

"Let's say you're right. You know as well as I do they's many a folk come from a black momma and a white daddy. Are those folks a quarter ape? That's just nonsense."

"I said it before and I say it again Jim Henry, you believe what you want and I'll believe what I want. They's just different from us. They's wild and we have to keep 'em in their place. One might have killed Snag and one might kill any one of us 'less we're careful."

The constable sighed, "You men don't go getting' het up now about somethin' that didn't happen. I'm about as sure as I can be there weren't no colored shot Snag. But they could be a lot of folks gettin' hurt if that kinda talk keeps on. And I'd be obliged if you all would help calm things down, instead of stirrin' things up."

This pronouncement was met with silence.

After a moment Jim Henry took his leave saying, "Well, seems like I'm right much of a wet blanket here. So I guess I'll get on out and let you boys enjoy your talk about biology, and the Bible, and such. Hope to see you all at church tomorrow."

Unspoken was the hope that he could get through the weekend without getting hurt or hurting someone else.

* * *

After visiting the company store, the furniture store and the cotton gin, Jim Henry went home for an early lunch. As he entered,

Joann looked puzzled. "You're back early. Has something happened?"

"No, nothing's happened—yet. But when folks git off at noon things might start happenin'. I thought I'd eat a bite and be back to the square when folks start comin' outta the mill. We got anything a hungry man could eat?"

"Remember we're snacking 'til tonight. But there's cheese, crackers and some hard boiled eggs."

"That'll do. Just make me a strong pot of coffee. I'm fadin' already."

"You'll have to settle for sun tea. I'm not about to fire up that stove just to make you a pot of coffee."

Jim Henry sighed, "Okay."

The constable sat and rubbed his face with both hands, "God git me through this day—and tomorrow! When the mill starts up on Monday, the hot heads'll be too busy for mischief."

"Oh Lord, I hope they are!"

"They will be, you just wait and see."

Joann set out the food and tea. Jim Henry took a long drink of the tea; it was so sweet it was almost syrupy—just the way he liked it.

"Let's talk about somethin' else for a while. How's the WMU plans for the revival comin' along?"

"Pretty well. I expect the flyers'll be here first thing next week. We'll get them out; there'll be notices in the mill and the company store. There ought to be a good turn out."

After the couple sat for a while, Joann continued, "I do say though, I get pretty tired of Eloise Summie. She's in the WMU and she's supposed to be helping with the revival. She does mighty little her own self, but she gripes about everything someone else does. I expect she's just mad because she's not the committee's chairwoman."

"Well, you've always said she feels she's better than the rest of us. I guess she thinks nobody else ought to be in charge."

"That could be right, and maybe I ought to feel sorry for her. I think she must be unhappy all the time. Why else would she be so sour on the whole world?"

"You feel sorry for her if you want. I can't. But I can stay outta her way."

"You won't be able to stay 'out of her way' this evening. You know she'll be at Mr. Hames' dinner. She wouldn't miss it, because that's about as highfalutin' as things can get in this town."

"Well, I just prefer to be where ever she's not—when I can."

* * *

It was noon. There was a long whistle blast that could be heard on farms two miles away. The doors of the Boiling Springs Mill seemed to explode outward. Women, men and children, some just eight years old, had completed another sixty six hour work week. They were anxious to leave the noise and cotton dust of the mill behind—until six o'clock Monday morning.

Some of the men stopped just outside the mill to light a cigarette. Most however walked rapidly up the slight grade leading from the mill to the village square. Women hurried along, knowing full well their work day was not over; there was food to cook, washing to do, and mending to see to. A group of a dozen or so young boys literally ran up to the square. These were doffing boys, boys who removed full bobbins of thread from spinning frames, replacing them with empty ones. The boys ranged in age from nine to twelve. Unlike the adults, these boys still had energy to burn.

Three of the boys said goodbye to their mates and started walking north on Main Street, toward their homes. The remaining group wandered east, thirty yards or so past the cotton gin, to a spot just west of Puzzle Creek. They settled atop a short retaining wall. Below the wall lay a narrow grassy area, and then a street with no name running to an area of the village called The Flat. Several black men were digging a drainage ditch on the east side of this street. One of the boys produced a package of cigarettes and passed it around. The boys sat and watched the black men dig, and enjoyed the feeling of rebellion that came with smoking. In fact, smoking felt almost criminal. It was only ten years before that the Tennessee Supreme Court had upheld a total ban on cigarettes, ruling they were "not legitimate articles of commerce, being wholly noxious and deleterious to health."

Two of the younger village men, George Hollis, called Gee, and Howard Green, nicknamed Haw, came walking from the square along the path the boys had followed. Both men were of average height, thin and lanky. Jim Henry was probably not the only villager who, upon seeing them, immediately thought of ferrets. The pair went everywhere together, so much so that they were often referred to not as Gee and Haw, but collectively as GeeHaw. Where they went it was not uncommon for trouble to follow. Gee sat down beside the boys.

"Gimmie one of them smokes, boy."

Reluctantly the owner of the cigarettes handed over the pack. "They ain't free, you know."

"Hell, you can afford the cost of a few smokes. You're a workin' man."

Haw chimed in, "I bet you work harder than that lotta darkies down yonder. A white man'll work rings around a colored any day."

The black men took no notice of Haw and his remark. Gee added, careful to speak loudly enough for the black workers to hear, "A darkie ain't good for nothin' 'cept drinkin', gamblin', and makin' more darkies."

Several of the black men, R. D. and Gaston among them, looked over at the group, but continued working without making any comment.

One of the younger boys decided to display his bravado. "That's why they ain't no coloreds workin' in the cotton mills. If they wuz they wouldn't pull their weight and we'd all have to work that much harder."

R. D. stopped shoveling. "I rec .. I rec .. I reckon I ain't the one se .. se .. settin' round makin' fun at people what is workin'."

Gee yelled, "Don't you backtalk no white, you shiftless darkie."

At this point a lady passed by on her way from The Flat to the square and the company store. "You young 'uns ought to git on home and not be out here botherin' people tryin' to work."

One of the boys whined, “Aw, Miz Houser, we ain’t doin’ nothin’.”

“I know very well what you’re a-doin’, and you ought to git home. And GeeHaw you all ought to be ashamed. The example you’re a-settin’ for these young boys!”

Gee and Haw stared at Mrs. Houser, but made no response, and she continued on her way.

Gee felt that he had been belittled in front of the young boys. He yelled, “R. D. I rec .. I rec .. I reckon you talk about like you work—pretty damn sorry.”

Gaston murmured something to R. D. and the men continued with their work.

As time passed, the younger boys joined in, and the comments became more and more insulting, but the black men continued to ignore them.

Finally Haw could not stand being ignored. He picked up a rock and threw it at R. D.; the rock missed. Several of the black men stopped working and stared at the group atop the wall. Gaston said, “Don’t you folks be throwin’ no rocks down here. You might hurt somebody.”

Gee asked, “If we folks don’t want to stop, who’s gonna stop us?”

Jim Henry, approaching from the square on the road Mrs. Houser had taken, spoke up. “I expect I would be the one who’d have to do that.”

He walked to a point just below the white group and looked up at them.

“I want all you boys outta here right now. You young ‘uns know better than to act like this, and GeeHaw, you two actin’ like you weren’t as old as the young ‘uns.”

Gee smirked, “Constable Tate. You would stick up for these darkies. You must have some coloreds in yore family tree.”

“Gee, don’t try me. Just shut up and get on away from here.”

“Why ain’t you arrested the darkie what killed ole Snag? Ever body says Snag was beddin’ a colored gal and one of her kin killed him.

You got yoreself a black gal, constable?"

"I might be able to find who killed Snag if I didn't have to spend so much time with hotheads like you. Now are you goin' or not?"

Gee said, "I reckon not." And with that he jumped off the retaining wall toward the constable.

Jim Henry moved toward Gee as he jumped, and before Gee's feet were on the ground the constable struck him in the face with an open hand. Gee pivoted in the air and landed very nearly flat on his back. The wind was thoroughly knocked from him.

The constable stood over him. "Don't you git up from there 'til I tell you."

There was little danger Gee would rise soon. He flopped about on the ground trying to catch his breath. The young boys began slowly moving away, but Haw remained, embarrassed that he had let Gee jump at Jim Henry by himself, and embarrassed for Gee because the constable had decked him. But he lacked the grit to launch an attack.

"Haw, you git down here and see if you can help yer buddy get his wind. Then I want to see yore backside as you boys go on home. I don't have time to be messin' with the likes of you. And for God sake, grow up!"

"You had no reason to hit Gee like that, Jim Henry."

"Would you rather I'd shot him? He's damn lucky I got him down before he got to me. If he'd hit me I'd've had to take him to jail. As it is, I'm gonna forget about this when you two are gone."

Soon Gee was breathing normally and Haw helped him to his feet. Gee had had the starch taken completely out of him, but he was still angry.

"That nosy busybody Miz Houser sent you over here, didn't she?"

"How do you know I didn't smell you two and figure I ought to see what devilment you was brewin'? Anyhow, let me tell you what's what. If you don't begin to act like grown men somebody'll wind up havin' to shoot you. This struttin' around like a banty rooster makes you look a fool, and it's gonna git you in real trouble."

Jim Henry was sure the muttering he heard as the two moved away was mostly curses aimed at him.

* * *

Back in the square everything seemed to be normal. So Jim Henry went to spend time in the company store. He could not do much to further the murder investigation before evening; and he did have theft to deal with—theft that was almost surely coming from the menswear department. And, though the constable would not admit it, even to himself, prowling the company store allowed him to enjoy the presence of the beautiful milliner.

While Jim Henry was in the store everyone seemed to act suspiciously. Maybe they were just curious about his being armed. Perhaps that explained the continued looking over shoulders, the turning away when he looked at any employee directly.

Be that as it may, none of the menswear clerks appeared more nervous than any other employee. So, well before his target time of four o'clock, Jim Henry left the company store and made several tours around the square, behind the warehouses, and behind the gin. Then he walked over to the area near Puzzle Creek where the several black men had been working, and discovered they had finished work for the day, or else gone on to another job. Finally he went home to clean up and dress for the Hames' dinner.

As he entered the house, Joann called from the bedroom, "I hope that's you Jim Henry."

"It sure is. You expectin' somebody else?"

Jim Henry peeked in the bedroom to find his wife bathing. She smiled. He began to undress.

* * *

Joann rolled over, propped on her elbow and punched Jim Henry.

"Law Man, have you dropped off? I bet my bath water's cold. And I am gonna have to redo my bath."

Jim Henry merely grunted.

"You need to get up and put on your pants. You've got to get some more water and warm it up. I need it and you've got to clean up before we go up to Mr. Hames' house."

Jim Henry made a grab for his wife, but she rolled away. So, he obediently rose and pulled on his trousers. He went to the kitchen and added wood to the fire in the stove. He then fetched two buckets of water and put a kettle full on the stove. When the kettle began to whistle he filled a basin about half full of unheated water. Then boiling water from the kettle was added to the basin until the temperature of the water was comfortably warm. This basin he took in to Joann. He kissed her and began to fondle her breast.

"Get out of here Jim Henry. We don't have a lot of time. We need to get dressed and get to that dinner."

The constable returned to the kitchen and prepared a second basin for himself. After bathing, he slipped on clean pants, and took a fresh basin of hot water to the back porch where he shaved. Finally he got more water, and rinsed out both basins.

Joann called, "I have your coat and clean shirt laid out, and a tie that'll look good with the coat. You better get a move on."

Jim Henry put on the shirt and tie his wife had chosen. As he was putting on his shoes Joann asked, "Must you wear your revolver tonight?"

"Yes ma'am, I'm afraid so. I've made it through the day so far with no serious trouble—but the day ain't over. I know it makes you uncomfortable. It makes me right much more comfortable though. I'll have my coat on at Hames' place. Not many folks will notice. By the way, I want to stop at Broadus White's as we go up the street."

The cotton buyer's home was on the east side of Main Street, about half way between Forrest Hames' house and Jim Henry's. Broadus came to the door quickly in answer to the constable's knock.

"Evenin' Broadus. You goin' to Mr. Hames' dinner?"

"No, I think he's only havin' the store clerks—along with Harry and Miss Morgan of course."

"Well, I'd be grateful if you'd stay ready to go. If we're gonna have trouble I think it'll be this evenin'. The hell raisers have had time to take a drink or two by now."

"I don't have nowhere to go tonight. You just give a holler if need be."

"I will Broadus. And I'm obliged. Like I said, if you have some bird shot you might have it on hand along with yer four ten. I don't want you to have to do no shootin' that'd kill a body. But it might come to shootin'."

"I shore hope not."

"That makes two of us Broadus."

* * *

Forrest Hames was a widower, and his children were long since grown and gone. He lived alone in an eleven room house located on the highest point in the village. The houses in the village each sat on a lot that was an eighth of an acre, or less. Hames' home—along with a small cottage for his colored retainers, Maudie and Jubal Surratt, and a smaller storage building—occupied two acres.

Hames stood at the door of his house welcoming guests.

"Good evening constable. Mrs. Tate, I'm glad you were able to make it."

"Good evening Mr. Hames. It's always a pleasure to see you. Jim Henry and I know we'll enjoy you and your wonderful home."

"I understand young Jimmy is living away in Lawndale. You must miss him."

"We surely do. But he's living with his aunt so he can go to school there."

"I understand. The Piedmont School is said to be one of the very best."

"Yes, that's what we've heard."

"I have hopes we can have a high school in Boiling Springs

before too long."

"That would be great."

"Well, just go on through. We're in the yard this evening. Maudie and Jubal have set up several tables out back. Jim Henry, could I speak with you for a moment?"

Joann smiled at Forrest and left the two men alone.

"Thunderation, Jim Henry! Why is every single person in Boiling Springs talking about Snag being killed by one of our coloreds? I thought we weren't going to let on about Snag being involved with a colored woman."

"We didn't let on about it. But they was lots of folks knowed about Snag's fight with Rafer, and pretty soon word got out about the reason for the fight. I reckon it was Rafer who told that. I never did believe we could keep it quiet."

"This killin' has got to be wrapped up soon. Have you made any progress?"

"No sir. But I hope to tonight. Have you spoken to LuElla? Can I speak to her?"

"Yes, yes, I've said to her that it looks like somebody assaulted her. She denies it. But I still don't see ..."

Just then more guests arrived and Hames turned his attention to them. Jim Henry slipped away, and found Joann talking with Hoyle Kendrick.

"Hello Hoyle."

"Evenin', Jim Henry."

"Joann, I'll be right back, I need to speak to somebody before we eat."

"Alright dear. Don't you go hiding out and being stand-offish though."

Jim Henry went into the kitchen where Maudie and LuElla were putting large trays of biscuits into the ovens of two large stoves. "Evenin' Maudie, LuElla—how are you all tonight?"

"We're fine, Mr. Jim Henry. But we 'bout worked to death

gittin' all this food ready. Mr. Hames can't have just a few folks in. He don't know how to do nothin' 'less he's goin' at it whole hog."

"LuElla, when you finish with those biscuits, I want to talk to you a minute."

LuElla turned away from the constable, "Mr. Forrest say he was gonna talk with you. But I don't have nothin' to say, Mr. Jim Henry."

Maudie picked up two platters of country ham and started out the door. "I'm gonna start carryin' some a these things out. LuElla, you talk while you work. You got no time to be standin' 'round."

"LuElla, I know you're busy. But it seems somebody's treated you like a dog. I need to know who that was."

"Ain't nobody done nothin' to me. I just got the clumsies, and fell down them back steps at home."

"From the way you're hobblin' around, and the looks of yer face, you must've got up and fell down them steps another time or two. You expect me to believe that? The scoundrel that beat up on you needs to be in jail."

"Ain't nobody goin' to jail, cause ain't nobody done nothin' to me."

"You're busy now. But we're gonna talk about this again LuElla. I need to git to the bottom of this. You hear?"

"I hear, but I done told you what I'm gonna tell you."

Maudie came hustling back into the kitchen.

"Mr. Jim Henry, you terrible in the way. And LuElla, cut some more biscuits. We 'bout got Pharaoh's army to feed out yonder."

Jubal came in and began putting plates of sliced tomatoes on a large serving tray.

Jim Henry patted Maudie on the shoulder as he left.

"I'm outta yer kitchen Maudie. Excuse me for bein' in yore way."

Maudie snorted.

Jim Henry found Joann talking with Eloise Summie. Joann took Jim Henry's arm and rolled her eyes at him in a way he knew meant he should help her get away from Mrs. Summie. He just smiled at her.

"Good evening, constable. I was just asking your wife why we find you two here this evening. I thought this was for the retail staff and administrators."

Joann's fingers dug painfully into Jim Henry's arm.

Jim Henry chuckled, "I suppose Mr. Hames thought we looked hungry. I'm just mighty glad he invited us. This spread sure looks fit to eat." Turning to his wife he said, "Joann, I think I see a tub of ice tea over yonder. Let's us get a glass before we eat. We'll join you later, Eloise."

As they moved way, Joann fumed, "Why do we find you here? My Lord, that woman has such an exaggerated opinion of herself! I could just scratch her eyes out sometimes."

"Now, now sweetheart, you said yourself the other day that she was never satisfied. Maybe that's her problem."

"Don't try to be funny Jim Henry. I'm not in the mood."

Jim Henry knew when to back off. He walked his wife to the iced tea in silence, and used the dipper hanging on the side of the tub to fill two glasses. They then moved away toward the small storage building where no one was standing. Jim Henry thought a few minutes without polite chit-chat was called for.

After a bit Joann sighed. "I tell you Law Man, that woman gets my goat! She puts on such airs. And she's nosier than anybody I've ever seen. I'm sure she went through every room in Mr. Hames' house as she came through; she was even in this little storage shed before she latched onto me. I wouldn't be surprised if she went through Maudie and Jubal's house. What business is it of hers why we're here? What nerve!"

Jim Henry nodded in silence and looked over the group milling about the yard. He was thinking about the real reason they were invited. The company store theft certainly was not as important as the murder. But the theft had to be addressed.

"Joann, I need to set by Rat Tail. I'm workin', you know."

"What? Jim Henry, I can't sit by that woman!"

After a short pause Jim Henry sighed, "Okay, okay, then let's go over and attach ourselves to Byron Scruggs. He might know somethin' I could use."

The couple moved across the yard and joined Byron's group of four.

"Evenin' Byron. Who's your lady friend?"

"Oh, hello Jim Henry. This here's Nancy Hawkins. Nancy just moved to town and she's workin' in the drug section. Nancy, this is Joann and Jim Henry Tate. You'd best watch out 'cause Jim Henry's the constable."

"I'm right glad to meet you both."

"Where are you from Nancy?"

"Oh, I'm from Forest City."

"And where are you livin'?"

"I'm at Suitsus Cottage. It's a wonderful place, especially for a girl who's new to town. The other women have been so kind to me."

"I'm sure they have," Joann said. "We're very lucky to have such a nice rooming house for single women employed in the mill, the store, and the school."

"It is nice, and spacious. In addition to the bedrooms there's a large kitchen we can all use and a huge living room."

Jim Henry asked, "Ain't the retired sheriff and his wife managing the Cottage now?"

At this point Forrest Hames appeared from inside and rang the "dinner bell," which sat atop a pole just outside the back entrance to the kitchen. Forrest had brought the bell from his old family homestead not too far southwest of the village. Most every farm in the county—most likely every farm in the South—had just such a bell.

All conversation ceased and all eyes turned toward Hames.

"I want to welcome you all tonight. This evening we're not doing business, we're just enjoying ourselves. But of course I understand that it's you folks who're responsible for the successful business of the company store. The Boiling Springs Mill Store is the largest store in the county, and it brings in the most money year after year. And I'm mighty grateful to you all."

Polite applause followed.

"We're about to eat a wonderful meal—you all know what a cook Aunt Maudie is—but first, Preacher Tarleton, would you return thanks?"

Following the prayer Jim Henry followed Byron to a table, and with just a little pushing, found a seat beside him. Joann sat down beside her husband and pinched his leg—her signal that his pushing had not been as discreet as he'd hoped.

There were four tables—each one seating ten people. Each table was loaded with fried chicken, country ham (that wonderfully salty cured pork), and stew beef. Stew beef, a local dish, was simply a pot roast of beef without the vegetables. The beef was cooked until it was fork tender, then removed from the pot and shredded. A thick gravy was made in the stew pot; then the shredded meat was stirred into the gravy and the result seasoned heavily with black pepper.

In addition to the meats, there were platters of sliced tomatoes and pickles of all sorts, chopped raw onion and chow-chow. There were bowls of green beans, pinto beans, field peas, turnip greens and rice. Finally there were pones of cornbread and baskets of hot biscuits. These baskets would be constantly refilled by Jubal.

As plates were being passed around, Jim Henry asked, "Byron, I've been told that Snag Wiley visited the store's menswear section pretty often. Did you ever notice that?"

"Well now that you mention it, it does seem like Snag used to be around quite a lot."

"That's just a mite strange, 'cause I never saw Snag in nothin' but overalls and work shirts—if he was wearin' a shirt."

Byron nodded, "I guess it was strange. We have lots of people in and out though. Lots of folks just come in to look, 'cause they can't afford to buy."

Jim Henry said, "Yeah, that's true. But I don't see Snag as a man who liked to look at clothes, do you?"

"I reckon not. But, you know...hmmm."

Jim Henry ate some stew beef and rice. He hoped that Byron would continue.

Byron asked his date to pass him some chow-chow. She did and he put a large spoonful on his pinto beans, tasted them and then added some chopped onion. He ate for a while, turned to Jim Henry and said, "I wonder if Snag was kin to Rat Tail. Seems like Snag spent a lot of time talkin' with Rat Tail."

Jim Henry smiled, "I don't know. Maybe they was kin."

The constable thought he must thank Joann for refusing to sit with the Summies. He buttered two more biscuits.

Jim Henry tuned out the table talk, and lost himself in thought and food. There was reason to believe he was now a mite closer to solving the company store thefts. Did that mean he was closer to solving Snag's murder? He'd have to talk with Rat Tail. Did Rat Tail own a shotgun?

Just then Jubal tapped Jim Henry's shoulder and leaned down to softly say, "Mr. Jim Henry, Mose is out yonder by the kitchen door. He say he needs to speak with you. He say it's mighty, mighty important."

Jim Henry turned to Joann. "Jubal says Mose is wantin' to see me. I'll be right back." He said to his fellow diners, "You folks excuse me a minute," and walked to the kitchen door where Mose stood—obviously agitated.

"Evenin' Mose. You lookin' for me?"

"Mr. Jim Henry, you need to come to The Line right quick. They's gonna be trouble there. A buncha white boys headed up there lookin' for trouble. Trouble gonna find 'em, and find some black folks too."

Immediately Jim Henry said, "Mose, you go tell Broadus White to come to The Line quick as he can. Tell him to come like I said."

"Yes sir Cap'n."

"Tell 'em come 'like I said'—that part's important. Then you go tell Zeno Harris to meet me at The Line quick as he can. Get goin'

Mose—fast as you can move!"

Jim Henry hurried back to Joann.

"I've got trouble on The Line. Don't know when I'll be home. You take care."

The constable ran around to the front of the house and began running north along Main Street. Knowing that he could not move very fast along the railroad, he determined to go north along Main and then follow a short unnamed street west. This would bring him to the café located at the south end of the black section.

* * *

As he neared the café, Jim Henry was gasping for breath. He stopped, bent over with hands on knees, and stood panting. Becoming aware of angry yelling, he hurried toward the noise. First he saw only the backs of several white men. But as he moved closer, he could see there were two—no, three—people struggling. There was also a group of black men gathering. "Oh shit," he gasped, and tried to draw his revolver as he ran, but without success.

Jim Henry stopped, managed to un-holster his gun and fired into the air. The group of whites scattered a bit and looked at him as he now walked forward. He could see GeeHaw fighting with R. D., and beyond them were black men coming toward the white group.

"Ever body stay put! GeeHaw, you sons a bitches, back off!"

Continuing to walk toward the fight taking place, the constable pointed his revolver at the advancing blacks.

"You boys! I done told you to stay put!"

He reached the fight and attempted to use his weapon to club Gee, but he missed as all three men fell to the ground. He tried once again and managed to strike Gee a glancing blow. Both Gee and Haw were in the process of rolling away and getting to their feet. Jim Henry stopped cold in his tracks. R. D. was on the ground bleeding profusely. The black man attempted to rise but fell back to the ground. He appeared to have been cut several times, and most of his right ear was missing.

Jim Henry looked at the black men standing by.

"Elvy, you go git ... oh hell no! You can't run on that ankle of yourn. Somebody needs to run get Dr. Callahan and I mean fast! Move!"

One of the younger black men started but his way was blocked by the gathered whites. Now Jim Henry pointed his revolver at the white group.

"You men make way there! Let that boy through!"

The men moved aside and the black man dashed past and around the corner by the café. Only then did Jim Henry realize that GeeHaw had disappeared.

"God damn that pair," he yelled. Then, "All you men git back to yer homes. I'll wait here for the doctor."

But nobody moved.

"Ain't they been enough devilment to suit you? You want somebody else layin' there beside R. D. tryin' to bleed theirselves to death? Well, I might just oblige if you all push me enough."

The whites slowly began to drift apart and a few turned to leave. Just then Broadus White came running up with shotgun in hand. Both black and white eyed him suspiciously as he came and stood with the constable.

One of the white men yelled, "Broadus, you're just another damned company lackey!"

The cotton buyer merely saluted with his shotgun.

Jim Henry put his hand on White's shoulder and nodded. He then turned to the black group.

"Somebody get some rags or somethin'. We need to see if we can stop some of R. D.'s bleedin'. The doctor won't be here for a while. See if one of the ole grannies can come help out. Elvy, help me out here. Git somebody movin'."

Elvy turned to the black men and began giving orders. To one he said, "Go git Granny Foster. Tell her R. D. cut bad." To another he directed, "Git a quilt. And some clean rags." Then, "When de quilt come we'll move 'im to his house. He won't rest there but he'll be better off than he is on the ground."

The constable, yelling first at one group and then another, began again trying to get the men to disperse. But both groups were slow to leave and there was a constant rumble of complaints and curses. Jim Henry stood quietly for a time and then approached the black group.

"I'd be grateful if you boys would just back off and go on home. We're gonna see to R. D. and I got more help on the way. They's gonna be no more trouble tonight."

Slowly, the men began moving away, except for two who were squatting beside R. D. Jim Henry then approached the white group, which had thinned to less than ten. One of the men came forward.

"Why in hell ain't you arrested whichever darkie killed Snag? GeeHaw says you know one of 'em done it."

"Has any of you ever caught GeeHaw tellin' the truth about anything?" asked Broadus.

Jim Henry nodded and said, "Them two are ninety per cent mouth and ten per cent bluster. You all know that. I'm gonna find out who killed Snag. I'm near 'bout as sure as can be it weren't nobody on The Line. I'm damned sure I'm gonna come down on GeeHaw like a load of bricks."

"Well, they's white men anyway, and ready to stand up to a connivin' darkie. That's good enough for me."

"Connivin' darkie? R. D.? That's as good a colored man as you'll find anywhere. What happened here anyway? Why the hell was you boys anywhere close to The Line?"

No one answered.

"Alright. I expect you followed GeeHaw here. That pair was goin' after R. D. right about noon time. Did GeeHaw follow R. D.?"

"I reckon so," one man mumbled. "But R. D. done pulled a gun on Gee."

"What?"

Jim Henry turned and hurried back to where the black man lay. Sure enough, slightly under R. D.'s hip was a small revolver. He reached for the pistol thinking, why did I not see that? "R. D., what in hell're you doin' with this thing?"

The black man's eyes opened, he moaned, and looked away.

Jim Henry holstered his own weapon, and opened the gun he'd taken from R. D. There were five cartridges, all unfired, and one empty chamber. R. D. had apparently carried his revolver with the hammer resting on an empty chamber, as did most everyone.

Zeno Harris came huffing past the café, slowed to a walk and came to where R. D. lay.

"Oh my God! What happened here?"

"It was GeeHaw, them worthless shits. They've 'bout killed R. D. and run off. I don't know how this come about, but I'm gonna find out. Right now we need these men to go home before somebody else acts a fool."

Zeno nodded, "I'll take care of that." Zeno looked around. Some men were leaving, but others seemed determined to remain.

"All right, you men, you need to leave here and go on home. 'Course those of you that's ready to get fired and be thrown out of your house, just stay here while I take your names."

With that a slow exodus began.

Jim Henry grabbed Sam "Slim" Scruggs, a brother of Amos and Byron, and the youngest of the Scruggs clan.

"Slim, you ought to have better sense than to be out here. But since you are here, you just stay and tell me what all happened."

The young man was all but squirming with embarrassment.

"Aw, Jim Henry, I just wanted to see what was happenin'."

"Slim, right now we ain't talkin' about why you're dumb enough to be with that crowd. We're talkin' about how GeeHaw, and them that follows 'em around, got here—and how R. D. got cut up so bad."

"He did pull a gun on Gee, he did!"

"Yeah. But back up. Why was GeeHaw here on The Line?"

"Well, they was a bunch of us in the park—settin' round the band stand, you know. And, ... well, ... R. D. come walkin' along the tracks headed toward The Line. GeeHaw commenced to yell at him. But R. D. didn't pay no mind. So GeeHaw falls in behind R. D. and walks up the track behind him. And, well, I reckon we all just went along too."

"So you're all walkin' along the tracks. What then?"

"Then nothin'. R. D. just kept walkin'. But I guess maybe some others yelled some things at R. D. That didn't git no rise out of 'im though."

"Well somethin' must of got 'im riled if he pulled a gun."

"Oh, ... well, ... Gee begun to pretend he was stutterin'. R. D. just continued to pay Gee no mind, but when he got to the café I reckon he felt easier, safer you know, cause that's when he turned and begun to cuss GeeHaw. Well, Gee made a swing at R. D. and R. D. begun to run away. But he didn't run far till he turned and aimed that gun at Gee."

"But he didn't shoot."

"He tried! He snapped that pistol, maybe a couple times. But you know, that gun wouldn't shoot, and Gee made at R. D. with his knife. Now I don't think he cut 'im, cause then R. D. hit Gee a good 'un with his pistol. Gee was sort of stunned and R. D. kept a-clubbin' on 'im. That's when ole Haw jumped R. D. from behind and went at 'im with his knife. Then you showed up."

Jim Henry kicked the ground in frustration.

"God damn that pair! I ought to have arrested both of 'em when they was actin' up around noon time!"

The constable looked back to see several black men lifting R. D. onto a quilt. He sighed, "Damn, damn, and double damn! Slim, git yore little skinny butt home. And if you want to buddy with somebody, buddy with them that *is* somebody—not with a worthless crowd like this 'un tonight."

Jim Henry walked back to stand with Broadus and Zeno.

"I'm mighty obliged to both you fellers. Things might nigh got outta hand here."

The cotton buyer and the super merely nodded.

As the three men watched, R. D. was taken to a house some three doors down from where they stood. The group carrying him entered and a small, wrinkled and bent black woman came from the north end of the line, obviously headed for the same house.

Broadus said, "That must be Granny Foster. I hope she knows somethin' about healin'. It'll probably be a while yet 'fore Callie gets here."

Jim Henry snorted, "I reckon we've seen the last of GeeHaw. I'll look for 'em, but I'm bettin' they'll be in South Carolina before long. It's good riddance, but I hate R. D. had to git cut up like that."

Zeno looked around, "I'll send one of the night watchmen up here for the rest of the night. The other will have to patrol the mill by himself tonight."

"That's a good idea Zeno. I think the fire's about out now, but a feller never can tell."

* * *

Jim Henry made his way slowly down Main Street. He had no lantern and most houses were dark. The moon was near full, but a light cloud cover rendered it of very little use. The constable had intended to remain on The Line only until the doctor arrived, but he had stayed on, even after Dr. Callahan left, to see that the night watchman showed up. Then he had stood for a time outside R. D.'s house awaiting information, feeling out of place and unwelcome. Eventually Granny Foster had come out to sit on the front porch and invited him to sit with her. They had discussed R. D., and night had crept in almost unnoticed.

As he passed Hames' house, Jim Henry saw there was still light in one of the front rooms. The dinner was long over, but remembering the platters of food, the constable realized he was hungry. He had only begun his meal when it had been interrupted by Jubal. With hunger also came the fatigue that follows anger and adrenalin.

God damn it, he thought, I should've stopped this mayhem before it started. I could've stopped it. Then these thoughts were pushed aside by the even more depressing thought of Snag's murder—on which he had made no apparent progress. On top of that there was the theft—on which he might have inched along, but not far. Damn and blast, he thought. I'm the law in this town. It's my town and I'm not taking very good care of it. Suddenly the constable stopped in mid stride. Wait a minute! R. D.'s pistol misfired! Rafer's pistol misfired! How likely is that? Jim Henry turned and began walking back toward the line as rapidly as the darkness would allow.

When the constable arrived back at R. D.'s home, there were several black men sitting on the porch. There was a shotgun propped beside one of the men, and a couple others quickly hid something under their chairs. Jim Henry ignored the shotgun and pretended not to notice the hidden bottles. He understood the shotgun and he was not concerned about alcohol.

"How's R. D. doin'?"

"He still alive. But he bled a whole lot. Dr. Callahan won't say if he think R. D. gonna live or not."

"Is Granny Foster with 'im? I really need to ask 'im just one question."

"Cap'n, ain't ole R. D. had enough truck with white folks for a while? He probably asleep."

"I know, I know, and I'm awful sorry. But it's real important. They's something I shoulda asked before I left. I think I'm gonna have to insist."

After waiting for a moment, Jim Henry walked onto the porch and tapped lightly on the frame of the open door. He got no response, but he stepped just inside the door. There were three black women sitting in what served as the living room of the small cottage. He recognized Granny Foster and R. D.'s wife, Leona, but the third, younger, woman was unfamiliar to him.

"Evenin'. It's real important I talk to R. D. just for a minute. Wonder if I might step through?"

Granny Foster rose and went into an adjoining room. In only a moment she returned.

"He asleep. He really need to rest."

"I know that Granny, and I wish I didn't have to bother 'im. But they's a real important question, and I have to ask while I can."

"You mean before he die—if he die. Well, I reckon you can go on in. You are the law. And, seems to me like he'd be dead 'fore now if it won't for you."

Jim Henry went to R. D.'s bedside.

"Wake up R. D., it's me, Jim Henry."

There was no response, the constable shook the black man gently.

"R. D., R. D., wake up now. It's Jim Henry Tate."

R. D. opened his eyes.

"Cap'n, that you? What you ... what you want?"

"I need to know where you got yore pistol."

"You take my ... take my ... take my gun, Cap'n?"

"I did that, and I don't know if I can give it back or not. But where'd you git it R.D.?"

"I didn't st ... st ... steal it from no ... no ... nobody."

"Okay. You didn't steal it. I never reckoned you did. So where did you git it?"

"LuElla. I bou ... bou ... bought it from LuElla."

"Thanks R. D. I'm gittin' outta here now. You rest up and git well."

Jim Henry told everyone once again how sorry he was he'd had to bother R. D., and left The Line as quickly as possible. He needed to question LuElla, but unlike R. D., she was in no danger of dying; there would be time for that tomorrow.

DAY SEVEN

Jim Henry had arrived home late and talked with Joann until after midnight. He went over the fight, the escape of GeeHaw, and the discovery that the revolver R. D. had used was bought from LuElla and had—most likely—been Rafer's. He speculated that this revolver had been given to LuElla by Snag, who had carried it away from his fight with Rafer. Or, uncomfortable thought, had LuElla killed Snag and taken it? Surely not; he just couldn't see LuElla using a shotgun. In any event, he hoped LuElla would admit to her affair with Snag when she was confronted with the pistol. He needed to know when that relationship had been discovered.

After the couple had gone to bed, the constable continued this conversation—with himself—much of the night, as he lay unable to sleep. Finally sleep did come, but then almost immediately, it seemed, he woke to hear Joann calling from the kitchen.

"Jim Henry, are you going to sleep this whole day away? I'll have breakfast on the table in about ten minutes. We're having eggs with biscuits and gravy."

Jim Henry sat up, yawned and stretched. He felt pretty good. But then memory of the previous evening's events came flooding back. His good mood vanished. He feared this was going to be another bad day. He'd visit Rafer and verify that the pistol taken from R. D. was indeed his. He'd have to check on The Line, make sure there'd be a watchman there. He'd have to see if GeeHaw could be found. And still, he needed to talk with LuElla. With all the anger and fear raging up and down The Line, that would not be easy.

"Come on Monday!"

"What was that?"

"Nothin'. I'm just mutterin' to myself."

"Well, stop it. Do whatever you need to do, and get in here to eat. I didn't cook this just to throw it to the critters."

At breakfast Jim Henry recounted his plans for the day. He ended by saying, "I need to git up to The Line pretty quick, and with ever thing else I may not make it to church. You'd best go on without me."

Joann sighed, "I was afraid of that. I guess I'll have to speak to the Lord on your behalf." She took Jim Henry's hand, "And I'll say a word or two for R. D. He is gonna live, isn't he?"

"Like I said last night—or I guess it was this mornin'—I hope so. He lost a lotta blood, but if he don't git infected he ought to be all right after a while."

"Should I tell Rev. Tarleton about R. D.?"

"I don't see why not. R. D. needs all the help he can git. Help from the Lord would be right welcome."

The couple ate in silence for a time. Then Joann said, "You've left out one thing, Law Man. You better get up to see Forrest Hames in a hurry. He'll need to be told about the fight. If not, he'll explode when the news does get to him."

"Oh my Lord! That's right. Zeno might or might not have stopped in there last night. I'm pretty sure Broadus didn't. I've got to git to him first thing. 'Course he'll explode anyway, it'll just be a smaller explosion—I hope."

"When you see Mr. Hames, thank him again for such a pleasant evening. He put on a real feast. Too bad you had just started on your meal."

Jim Henry pushed away from the table. "Don't know when I'll

be back. It might be a couple hours or it might be dark."

"I know, I know. And I know another thing Law Man, you're going to the revival that's coming up no matter who's knifing who or who's killing who."

He gave Joann a kiss.

"Yes ma'am."

* * *

Jubal came to the door in answer to Jim Henry's knock.

"Mornin' Mr. Jim Henry. Seem like you had some trouble last night."

"So you know about R. D. Has Mr. Hames heard yet?"

"No Cap'n, I didn't think it was my place to tell 'im. Only way I know is from Granny Foster. Her and Maudie is kin. She sent a young 'un over to tell Maudie all about it."

"Can I see him, Jubal? He's got to know."

"He's in that front room what he use for his office at home. You go on in."

Jim Henry stopped at the door to the room where Hames sat at a small desk, busy with paper work. When Jim Henry rapped on the door frame, Hames looked up.

"Constable. I'm glad to see you. I couldn't fail to notice you leaving my dinner last night. You left in somewhat of a hurry. I expected you to report back to me before you went home last evening. Why didn't you?"

"I was tied up 'til very late. I thought you might be sleepin' by the time I got things sort of straightened out."

"Well, you're here now. Let's hear it."

"I guess you know, or you've heard of, George Hollis and Howard Green."

"Yes, but I don't believe I've heard anything good about them."

"They're not a good lot, that's for sure. And, well, on The Line last night they cut up R. D. pretty bad."

"Thunderation, Constable! I won't have such carrying on!"

Jim Henry put up his hands, palms toward Hames as if to hold him off. "I know, I know. I have to tell you we could've had a terrible set-to on The Line. But Broadus and Zeno stepped up to help me out and I think things're calmed down now."

Hames was not to be placated. "So you say, but the whole village seems to think one of our coloreds killed Zebulon Wiley. That's what's got everybody riled up, and it's what caused this ruckus. Arrest Rafer Jones and charge him with murder!"

"Mr. Hames, you might be right about folks bein' riled, but I'm not real sure last night's ruckus had a tie in to Snag's killin'. You ought to know that GeeHaw's just a bad pair. They might've cut up R. D. even if Snag had never been killed."

Hames snorted, and Jim Henry continued. "And you did give me 'til Thursday to find whoever killed him. Just let me tell you some more about last night."

After Jim Henry had gone through the events of the previous evening in great detail, Hames was in a cold fury.

"I tell you Constable, I'm going to see that we have no more of this. The houses occupied by the Hollis family and the Green family will be called for immediately." Hames stopped, shook his head and said, "No, the houses will be called for on Monday. I don't want folks thrown out of their homes on a Sunday. But come Monday, everybody in those houses will be requested to leave town at once! You see that they do it Constable."

"That's mighty hard Mr. Hames."

"I mean it to be hard! Peaceful folks—black or white—will not be attacked in my town! Now, what are you doing to keep the peace? When people get stirred up they're likely to do stupid things."

"Zeno had a watchman on The Line all night. I'll check by several times today, and we'll have a watchman there again later on. If we can make it through 'til Monday, things'll calm down. When folks go back to work they'll be too busy to think about fightin' and such."

"That sounds all right. Now you see to it. And remember, I want this murder wrapped up by Thursday one way or another. I won't have my town torn up like this."

Jim Henry had obviously been dismissed, and he was not unhappy about that. He could certainly do things more productive than listen to Forrest Hames ranting and raving. Joann could thank Hames for the dinner herself whenever she saw him next.

* * *

At Rafer Jones' house there seemed to be no one stirring. Jim Henry rapped on the door long and loud. Finally Rafer appeared. He was barefoot and wore only a faded and frayed pair of overalls.

"Good God, Jim Henry! Can't a man sleep on a Sunday morning? What do you want?"

"I don't want to arrest you and take you off to jail. You oughta be happy about that."

"Well, let me dance a little jig. That makes me a whole lot happier about bein' dragged outta bed by the local law."

Jim Henry held out the revolver he had taken from R. D.

"You can git back to bed Rafer, after you tell me if you know this pistol."

Rafer took the revolver and looked it over. He handed it back to the constable.

"Jim Henry, you know damn well that's my junky ole gun. I didn't know where it got to. Where'd you git it?"

"I don't reckon you need to know that, Rafer. I thought it was yourn, and I'm obliged to you for tellin' me I was right."

"Fine! Now go away and leave me be."

"I'll do that Rafer, but I'm afraid you're gonna see me again. Go on back to sleep."

* * *

When he arrived at The Line, some few people were beginning to come out and move toward the little black church. He saw no watchman, but this was not cause for concern. No one had told the watchman to remain after daybreak. What did cause concern was the number of black men carrying a shotgun or a rifle. He was sure this would be inflammatory, but he saw no way to force the men to put down their arms. At least for now, he'd let sleeping dogs lie. If any real trouble occurred it would probably be later. The white hell-raising contingent was probably still sleeping off their partying of the night before. He hoped this was true of any black hell-raisers as well.

Everyone noticed Jim Henry, as they would have any time he appeared on The Line. Some ignored him, others nodded, but his reception was decidedly cool and the air virtually crackled with tension. The constable devoutly hoped that GeeHaw was away from The Line to stay. It would only take one fool to set off a small race war in Boiling Springs. He turned and walked back the way he had come. Once clear of The Line he picked up his pace, and headed directly for Hames' home. Jim Henry caught the mill owner just as he left for church.

"Mr. Hames, we need to talk again for a minute or two."

"What is it constable? The men's Bible class is meeting in just a few minutes, and I intend to be there."

"The Line's like a tinder box this mornin'. It'll only take one tom-fool act by some white—or black—to set bullets a-flying. We need watchmen around right now to keep hot heads off The Line. I'll talk to Zeno about that, with yore okay."

"Yes, yes, of course. You tell Zeno I want watchmen up to The Line. If they have to leave the mill empty to do that, then so be it."

Hames shook his finger at Jim Henry. "And tomorrow constable, you just see the notices I'll have posted at the mill, the company store, everywhere! I'm not having this cutting and killing in my town!"

"Thanks Mr. Hames. I'll go talk to Zeno and let you git on to your Bible class."

Jim Henry began to stride rapidly toward the super's house.

Superintendent Zeno Harris was not rushing off to the men's

Bible class. He was dressed for church. But Jim Henry found him sitting on his front porch drinking coffee and smoking a cigar.

"Hello Zeno. Thanks again for the help last night. We could've had a bad situation. 'Course it's bad enough for R. D. I guess he's still alive; I ain't heard no different."

Harris nodded, "Yes, R. D. is a good colored man. I hope he recovers. I'm sure Callie will do everything possible for him."

"They still may be trouble though. Lots of the coloreds are goin' armed today. We need to see to it nobody goes in there and stirs things up worse than they already are. Could you git in touch with the watchmen and see to it that they's somebody on The Line right away?"

Zeno nodded and Jim Henry continued, "Well, maybe we need watchmen at both ends of The Line and not actually on it. We just need to keep hot heads outta there a while longer. Mr. Hames says if we need to leave the mill without any watchmen, that's fine."

Zeno put down his coffee cup, went to his front door, and yelled in, "I'm going across to the mill—back in a minute or so."

The constable moved back toward the street.

"And Zeno, if any of the watchmen run into Gee or Haw they should hold the son of a bitch and let me know."

"Don't worry, Jim Henry. I'll go over and catch one of the watchmen. I'll tell him to be sure two people are watching The Line the rest of the day and to be on the lookout for those two. Let me know if you need me again."

"I appreciate yer help. I'm goin' back up to The Line right now."

* * *

As Jim Henry approached R. D.'s home, he noted that while there were still black men sitting on the porch, there were now two shotguns. At least no alcohol was in evidence.

"Mornin' boys. How's R. D. doin'?"

The black men just stared. Apparently each was waiting for another to speak. Jim Henry became really uncomfortable with the silence.

"I'm gittin' no answer. I hope that don't mean he died in the night."

After a long pause one man spoke up. "No, he still alive. But he ain't no more than that—just alive."

"Dr. Callahan been by this mornin'?"

"No, but Granny Foster been with R. D. all night."

"I'm glad R. D.'s still with us. I won't bother him. I'm just gonna walk around for a while. Maybe I'll go over to the church. You boys goin' to church, or you gonna stay here?"

No one answered. The constable just nodded, turned and started toward the little church.

Walking along, Jim Henry tried to think how he could approach LuElla. He certainly did not want to worsen the already volatile situation on The Line. He also did not want to make LuElla's situation with her father any worse than it appeared to be. But damn it, there was just a possibility LuElla had killed Snag. That's one way she could have gotten the pistol. He didn't believe that was the case, but he had to consider it.

As he neared the church, Jim Henry saw Mose walking ahead of him. He ran toward the black minister and called, "Mose, you got time to talk with me?"

The black pastor turned and waited for Jim Henry to reach him.

"Mr. Jim Henry. God was wid you last night. Lot of peoples mighta wound up like R. D., or worse."

"I reckon God had a little help from me—and you. You're the one come and got me. You're a good man Mose. You helped me and lots of other folks yesterday." Jim Henry laid his hand on the black man's shoulder. "Now I need you to help me again."

"How's that Cap'n?"

"I'm bettin' you know I need to talk to LuElla."

Mose stood silent and looked past Jim Henry.

"I could just walk into her house and start askin' questions. Or I could arrest her and take her to the county jail and talk to her there. The way things are on The Line though, either way I might get a bunch of colored folks hurt, or I might get hurt. Or both them things might happen."

Mose nodded, "Yes sir, Mr. Jim Henry. I can see that."

"So I don't wanna do neither one."

"Yes sir."

"And—if I figure this right—I need to talk to LuElla without rilin' her daddy up any more."

Mose looked at the ground.

"What's this have to do with me, Mr. Jim Henry?"

"I might just know how to talk to her without raising any trouble. I want you to speak to LuElla. Tell her to stay around after church; think of somethin' to talk to her about after the service. Talk to her long enough so she'll leave church after most ever body else is well away from there. I'll wait outside and when she leaves I'll walk along with her. That way I can talk to her out in public, so nobody'll be suspicious of anything, but at the same time nobody can hear what we're sayin'."

Mose shook his head. "I don't know, Cap'n."

"Mose, R. D. says LuElla sold him that sorry pistol he had last night. That was Rafer Jones' pistol. I'm sure Snag took it the night he beat Rafer so bad. Now how could LuElla have got that pistol? She could have killed Snag and took it."

"She didn't do that, Cap'n!"

"I don't think she did. But I've got to find out how she did git that gun. Don't you see? I've got pretty good reason to arrest her right now."

After a long pause Mose sighed and softly said, "Don't do that, Mr. Jim Henry. I'll do like you say—if I can."

"Thank you Mose. I'll wander around The Line and then come sit outside the church somewhere. I'll just wait and see if LuElla comes out alone."

Mose looked toward the church. Then he looked at the ground. Finally he said, "Yes sir," and walked away.

Jim Henry walked the length of The Line and sat outside the

café. Soon a watchman came walking down the railroad, and the constable went out to meet him.

"Glad to see you. I think it'd be a good idea for you to stay around the corner. That way folks on The Line won't be as likely to see you, but you can see anybody comin' along the railroad or down from Main Street."

The watchman agreed and Jim Henry walked back to the church at the north end of The Line. Sure enough, there was a second watchman just east of the church. Jim Henry waved and the watchman lifted his arm in salute. The constable walked over to the west of the church and sat in the shade of some large pine trees. For ten minutes or so he watched as stragglers filed into church; soon then he heard singing. There followed a time when Jim Henry could make out essentially no words coming from inside the church. There would be brief periods in which he could hear only a murmur, followed by a chorus of "Amen!" This meant members of the congregation were testifying.

After a considerable time of testifying, there was more singing. This time Jim Henry could make out the song. First the leader sang, "Swing low sweet chariot." Then the chorus sang, "Comin' for to carry me home." The leader sang a different refrain, followed by the chorus singing, "Comin' for to carry me home." The hymn went on and on, with the chorus never changing. Jim Henry hummed along.

After several more songs the sermon began. The constable was unable to make out the words of the sermon. All he could hear was the rising and falling cadence of Mose's delivery, "da da da, DA … DA DA DA, … da da da, DA … DA DA DA." Jim Henry smiled. He had heard many sermons given by many black preachers. The pattern seemed never to vary. "Give 'em hell, Mose," he murmured.

* * *

Jim Henry was awakened by his head falling to the side. Momentarily he did not know where he was. But quickly he remembered. Sleep had eluded the constable for much of the preceding night and Mose's sermon had been long. In spite of the uncomfortable pine bark against his back, he had dozed off waiting for the exodus from the little black church. He stood and stretched. His left shoulder decided to complain again about the blow received on Wednesday.

A large number of folks were leaving the church, but Jim Henry could not see LuElla. He hoped she was still inside and that Mose was keeping her there. Since he wanted to be as inconspicuous as possible, the constable made no move toward the church. The stream of people leaving the church became a trickle, and then only the random one or two persons. Jim Henry now moved toward the church.

The small building sat on a low knoll with stone steps going from street level up to the church. Jim Henry waited just at the bottom of the steps and several yards to the west. For a minute or more no one else came out. He wondered again if LuElla was inside or if she'd left before he awoke. He began to pace back and forth. Then he saw LuElla emerge from the front of the church.

LuElla saw the constable at the same time he saw her. She stopped and looked back at the church. Jim Henry could see her droop. Then she threw her shoulders back and headed for the steps. The constable walked to meet her.

"LuElla, I didn't have much chance to talk with you last night. Today it's right much more important you tell me some things."

"I ain't got nothin' to say to you, Mr. Jim Henry."

She began to move away.

"That can't be so, LuElla. It's different today. If you don't talk to me I'll have to arrest you. I don't want that. I don't think you want it neither."

"Why you think you gonna arrest me?"

"Because you had Snag's gun. You might've got it when you shot him. Is they a twelve gauge shotgun in yore house LuElla?"

LuElla stopped. Her face showed both anger and fear.

"I ain't shot nobody."

"Maybe not. How'd you get Snag's gun?"

"Who says I had that gun? I ain't got no gun."

"R. D. says you sold him Snag's gun. Now I have it. Snag got it from Rafer Jones. Rafer says it sure is the gun he had the night of his brawl with Snag. How'd you git that pistol, LuElla?"

Tears began to form in LuElla's eyes.

"Well shit! Damn! That worthless white man give it to me."

"Why would he do that?"

Tears coursed down her cheeks.

"Cause he said he didn't have no money to give me."

Jim Henry gave LuElla a minute to compose herself.

"So it was yer daddy beat you. You was meetin' Snag down by the river. He was payin' you and yer daddy found out. Is that the way of it?"

LuElla stood for a minute lookin' down The Line.

"Mr. Jim Henry, you don't know nothin' 'bout what it's like to be colored. So you can't reckon what it's like to be colored in this little ole town! No you can't! My daddy won't even let me go down to the café to dance a little on a Saturday night. They ain't nowhere off The Line I can go, 'less I go there to wait on white folks. This Line is a mighty little place. I want to go Some Place! I want to do Somethin'—'cept cook and wash and wait on folks."

She sighed and brushed a tear away.

"If I has to spread my legs to the likes of that white trash to git away from here, I do it! I hear they's places in Charleston and Savannah, maybe even Charlotte, that's like a whole colored town. They's colored stores, colored cafés; ever thing. Colored theaters; stuff even white folks don't have here. You can be somebody there! I was gonna go. I just needed money."

"When did yer daddy find out about you and Snag?"

"Tuesday. He found where I hid my money. He took it all." She shook her head. "I was 'bout ready to leave."

"When's the last time you saw Snag?"

"I reckon it was the Thursday 'fore he got kilt."

"He give you the pistol then?"

"Yeah. I reckon he did."

"But normally he'd give you money?"

"Yeah. And if you want to know, it won't much—just a dollar or two." New tears formed in her eyes. "I had twenty seven dollars and thirty cents. Now daddy got it all. He say he gonna give it to the church. Church ain't got no need for that money."

Jim Henry waited again for LuElla to gather herself.

"When did you sell R. D. the pistol?"

"Friday a week ago—just 'fore that worthless white man wuz shot. The day after I got it."

Jim Henry walked along with LuElla. He knew in a few minutes he would have to leave her, and he knew there were more things he should ask. But what things? At first nothing came to mind—then something did.

"When did you first start meetin' up with Snag?"

"It musta been 'bout the middle of March. I know one time it was awful cold."

They were now well into The Line and near LuElla's home. Jim Henry stopped.

"You go on LuElla. And thank you."

She made no reply.

The constable realized he was very hungry. But he felt he shouldn't leave immediately after talking with LuElla. That would make their conversation seem important to anyone who had seen them. He looked around for someone else to speak with. It seemed however, that all residents of The Line were inside. No doubt they had left church hungry and were now eating, or preparing, their Sunday dinner. What to do? He decided to check on R. D. again.

There was only one young black man—hardly more than a boy—on the porch at R. D.'s, and no weapon was in sight. The front door was open, and nodding to the young man, Jim Henry stepped up and rapped on the door frame. A girl in her teens came to the door.

"Yes sir, Mr. Jim Henry?"

"Just wanted to check on R. D. again. How's he doin'?"

"Granny say he runnin' some fever. He sleep most of the time. When he awake he can't stay awake, can't do nothin'."

"I'm right sorry. I'll go see if Dr. Callahan can't come by right away."

Both because it gave him an excuse to leave promptly, and because he was worried that R. D. might not live, Jim Henry walked as fast as he could down the railroad toward the village square.

* * *

As Jim Henry was approaching Callahan's house, he saw the doctor climbing up into his buggy with bag in hand. The constable hailed him and Dr. Callahan stepped back down from the buggy and waited.

"Hello Callie. You headed to The Line?"

"Yep. Gonna look in on R. D."

"That's good. I was just there and they say he's running a fever."

"I'm not surprised. He lost a lot of blood, but infection is his biggest problem now. In a way R. D.'s lucky though. It looks like Haw had one of those hawk bill knives they use in the mill to cut yarn off bobbins and warps. Those things slash something terrible, but they have no point so you can't stab with them."

"I reckon you mean stab wounds are worse to get infected?"

"Very much so. Last night I bathed all his cuts in alcohol and sewed up the major ones. There may be nothing more can be done except to keep giving him lots of fluids. But I'll do what I can."

Jim Henry watched as the doctor climbed into the buggy and drove away. Then he turned and headed for home.

As he walked along, Jim Henry did some arithmetic. There had been thirty three dollars hidden in Snag's Bible. Of the money LuElla had hidden from her father, most—maybe all, of it—say twenty five dollars anyway—had come from Snag. That made fifty eight dollars Snag had scraped together from somewhere. Had it all been stolen from the company store? If so, Snag was not splitting evenly with his partner, for the loot had only amounted to about seventy seven dollars.

But maybe, he thought, I can look at it another way. Snag had been paying LuElla for sex for maybe sixteen weeks. In that time Snag would have earned, maybe, a hundred dollars honestly. But the man threw money away with both hands, mostly by drinking and gambling. He had to pay rent on his house, and he had to eat. He must have needed near eighty dollars in that period just to survive. If he had given LuElla twenty five, then he was short five, and that left nothing for Snag's other vices. Then there was also the money in Snag's Bible. Snag had to be paying LuElla with stolen money. Didn't he?

In frustration, the constable decided he could not decide, not just yet. But his instincts told him Snag was taking money from the company store. He had a partner, most likely Rat Tail, and Rat Tail was keeping almost none of the stolen funds. How could that be? Had Snag been doing something for Rat Tail? Was it something that was crooked?

Jim Henry sighed dejectedly. He muttered, "I ain't makin' no progress at all!"

* * *

At home, Jim Henry called out as he entered, "Is they any food for a hard workin' man?"

"There was a long while ago, but I threw it out since nobody was around to eat it."

"I hope you're funnin' me."

"Well sort of. I didn't know when you'd be back, so I made do with peanut butter, crackers and a glass of milk. There's cold biscuits and cheese. You come eat that and maybe some tomatoes. While you're at that I'll stir up the fire and scramble you a few eggs."

"That'll do."

"If you think you'll be home for supper I'll cook country ham, bake some fresh biscuits and make some red eye gravy this evening. You missed out on that last night." Joann sighed, "My, that was a good meal!"

"I do plan to be home. I'm just gonna check to see if GeeHaw's anywhere to be found. Then I'll make another check up on The Line, walk around and see if things are calmin' down. Don't know if I can do much more today."

The constable sliced some cheese and placed the slice in a biscuit.

"How'd things go at church?"

"Same as usual. But I bet you want to know if the preacher said anything about R. D."

"Yep."

"He did. He did a real good job. You know he always says something about the people who are sick, or in some sort of trouble—people needing help."

"He always does that."

"Well, he included R. D. He said there'd been some trouble on The Line and a peaceable, law abiding colored man had been cut up real bad. He said R. D. was near death, and said a prayer for him. After that he asked everybody to pray for R. D. Some were taken aback, but I think decent folks are going to do just that."

About then, thunder sounded in the distance.

"Did the preacher pray for rain? Wish I'd asked him to. If it begins to rain people'll stay inside. That'd be a good thing."

As he ate, Jim Henry told Joann about his conversation with LuElla. Then he told her his ideas about Snag being partnered with Rat Tail—stealing from the company store. He explained that it looked as if Snag had the upper hand in that partnership. And he wondered why.

"Or do I have it all wrong?" he asked.

"No, I don't think so. It sounds to me like Snag had something on Rat Tail. I bet he was blackmailing him."

"Yeah, he might've been. But what could it be? Rat Tail don't seem like no hell raiser. Maybe he was stealin' all along and somehow Snag found out."

"Could be, but does it really seem that Rat Tail would be stealing without some powerful reason—like blackmail?"

"I think I need to look real careful at Rat Tail."

"Well, you might look at Eloise too. I never have felt right about that woman."

* * *

Jim Henry walked onto the porch of George "Gee" Hollis' home. The front door was closed. In the July heat, this no doubt indicated no one was home. Nonetheless he rapped loudly, with no result. After rapping a second time the constable turned to leave. Just as he stepped off the porch, a Hollis neighbor came walking by.

"They's nobody home, Jim Henry. They're all gone to church."

"You reckon? Ain't church over by now?"

"Well, most places I guess so. But them Hollises walk all the way past Sunshine to that brush arbor meetin' place. They're gone near 'bout all day."

"Oh yeah. That's a Holiness group that meets over there, ain't it?"

"Yep."

"I guess then I'll just move along. I'm tryin' to find Gee. You seen him around?"

"Not today. And the cat's done out, Jim Henry. I know you're lookin' to arrest Gee 'cause him and Haw cut up ole R. D."

"News travels fast don't it?"

"Bad news shorely does."

At the home of Howard "Haw" Green the constable's luck was no better. Howard's mother was dead. He lived—most likely *had lived,* for he was probably long gone—with his father and two teen age brothers. The younger of the brothers was on the front porch. Jim Henry put one foot on the edge of the porch and leaned with his forearms on his knee.

"How're you Otis?"

The boy answered with a sneer, "I'm right tolerable, not that you give a good God Damn."

There's another one who'll do no good, thought Jim Henry. But he smiled and said, "You must know I'm lookin' for Haw. Is he around?"

"No he ain't. He didn't come home last night."

"You reckon I could just look inside and see for myself?"

The boy chuckled, "Well paw's asleep inside and wakin' him up 'cause you're callin' me a liar might git yore hair parted with a bush ax. Does that answer yore question?"

Jim Henry stared at the youngster. He swallowed and took a deep breath. He thought of several actions that he would have found very satisfying. But they would get him no nearer finding Haw. So he merely said, "You might ought to work on yore manners Otis," and turned and headed toward the village square.

* * *

Those few loafers around the square swore they had seen neither Gee nor Haw. So Jim Henry walked around to the back of the company store and began to follow the railroad toward the black section. As he walked up the railroad a light, misty rain began, and by the time he reached The Line the rain was moderate and steady. Jim Henry was happy it was raining, and happy Joann had insisted he wear a raincoat.

The watchman stationed at the south end of The Line was huddled under a scrub tree, trying to avoid at least the worst of the rain. Jim Henry walked over to him.

"If you can stand it, stay on a little longer. But if they's no sign of the rain lettin' up, I think you can go on about yer business."

"Okay, Jim Henry. They's been no comin' nor goin' so far today."

"I'm right happy about that."

The constable walked to the north end of The Line and had a similar conversation with the watchman there. He then doubled back to the small house where R. D. lived. This time there was no one on the porch, and when Jim Henry rapped the teen age girl he had seen earlier came to the door again.

"I see the porch is empty. That good news or bad news? How's R. D. doing?"

"He pretty much holdin' on. Dr. Callahan say chances he gonna live is better now than last night."

Jim Henry stood on the porch for a moment, and the girl stood silently looking at him.

"Well, that's great. Guess I'll go on then. If he's awake, you tell him lotsa folks prayin' for 'im."

"Yes sir, Mr. Jim Henry. I will."

The constable could think of nothing more he could do in the black quarter.

* * *

Walking down the railroad toward the village square, Jim Henry tried to think of how he might use the remainder of the day to accomplish something—anything. He was not ready to meet Rat Tail head on with questions about Snag, shotguns, theft, and the like. Due to the rain there were few, perhaps no, places where people would likely congregate. There would be no evening church services, because the pastor had responsibility for three separate churches. He held early service at one church, midday service at another, and evening service at a third. Boiling Springs currently had service midday; nearby Caroleen had evening service.

The rain was now coming down heavily. Jim Henry's raincoat was thoroughly soaked and doing little to keep him dry. He ran the last few yards to the bandstand and ducked in. The bandstand had no sides, but the rain was coming more or less straight down, and under the small structure's roof, it was dry.

Jim Henry took off his rain coat and shook as much water off it as he could. There was nowhere he could hang the coat to dry a little, so he laid it flat on the floor and sat down beside the coat. As the rain continued, the constable looked out at the railroad along which he had come and thought of R. D. coming up from the village square along that same road not quite twenty four hours before. "That damned pair GeeHaw," he muttered. And then he wondered, could it be that one, or both, of them had killed Snag? They were just exactly the sort that would have had to test the old "cock of the walk." They could easily be among those Snag had slapped down at the little beer joint. But were they really capable of murder? If so, why would they go after Snag at this particular time? After following this line of thought for a while, Jim Henry turned and looked to the east.

Less than thirty yards east of the bandstand stood the home of Rat Tail and Eloise. Though he had not considered it before, Jim Henry saw that anyone could leave Rat Tail's, cross the railroad, walk by the bandstand, and very quickly reach the path leading north along the river. Once somebody moved up that path even a few feet, they could only be seen by someone on the river bank, and then only if that someone was in a position to look due north along the path.

The constable looked north and south. He estimated that if you were to move from Rat Tail's to the riverside path, that movement could be observed from only five or six houses at most—more likely only four. So even in broad daylight it was very likely a rapid movement from Rat Tail's to the path—or vice versa—would go unnoticed. At dusk, or on a moonlit night, it would be almost certain no one would notice. It was clear, Jim Henry thought, that Rat Tail could have met Snag along the river and killed him there.

Suddenly the constable began to laugh. "Of course," he muttered. "How could I not see that?" He stood up, put on his raincoat, and struck out purposefully for home.

* * *

As he entered his home, Jim Henry called, "Joann! Joann! I've got it. I know who killed Snag!"

"Good! Go back on the porch and take off your shoes and that coat. You're tracking mud and dripping water everywhere."

Chagrined, the constable turned, went out, sat in the porch

swing and took off his shoes. He then removed his coat and shook it out. There was no place on the front porch to hang the coat, so he rolled it up, went through the house, and hung the coat just outside the kitchen door on the back porch. Then he went back in.

"Well. Now don't you want to know what I've figured?"

"Of course I do." Joann handed Jim Henry a towel. "Tell me while you dry your hair."

"Alright, you remember we thought Snag was shot by a body standing below him? I was real bothered when I couldn't find a place along the river bank where that could've happened."

"I remember."

"But here's how it went. Rat Tail must've met Snag down by the river. They had a fallin' out about their scheme at the company store. Snag hits ole Rat Tail one. Rat Tail falls and layin' there on the ground he shoots Snag. See, the shot's travellin' up as it hits Snag."

Joann chuckled.

"Jim Henry, you mean Snag hits Rat Tail who's standing right there in front of him holding a shotgun? And then Snag just stands there facing Rat Tail, who's got the shotgun, while Rat Tail shoots him?"

"Oh ... well ... but see, Rat Tail had that bruise on his face Monday. I told you. And Snag weren't too bright."

"I love you, Law Man. But that idea needs work." Joann stood and looked at Jim Henry for a moment and then continued, "And try this on. If somebody was on the ground shooting upward at Snag, I can think of who it might've been."

"Who?"

"Lying? On the ground? With Snag around? What did you tell me just a while ago? Think about it—LuElla, of course."

Jim Henry sighed. He sat in his favorite rocker and rubbed the towel over his head and face.

"You're right."

The constable rocked back and forth several times.

"But that don't mean I'm wrong. Rat Tail might've done it. I'm gonna have to look real careful at that old son."

"Well, you don't have to do it right now. The rain's letting up but it looks like it's going to be a steady drizzle for some while yet. Folks are going to stay in. Can't you take off what's left of the day?"

"I reckon I can." He leaned back and closed his eyes. "I remember somethin' about some country ham."

DAY EIGHT

Jim Henry had gone to bed untroubled and with a full stomach. He had slept soundly. At six o'clock Monday morning he woke feeling much refreshed and optimistic. While he had no clear idea how to go about it, he knew he was going to find out a lot more about Mr. Ralph "Rat Tail" Summie. And that "lot more," he was sure, would prove Rat Tail had killed Mr. Zebulon "Snag" Wiley.

The constable pulled on his pants and went into the kitchen where Joann was cutting slices of livermush.

"It's not gonna be a feast this mornin' Law Man. Just grits and livermush. It's Monday you know. There's washing to be done, and I've got to be at the church pretty soon. Our flyers are due to come in and we'll be delivering soon as we get them."

"A man can't complain about grits and livermush."

The constable went out to the back porch and looked at the morning sky. "Looks like it's gonna be a sunny day." He headed for the privy. "I'll be back in a minute."

After breakfast Jim Henry headed for The Line. He wanted to see if things were quiet there, and to check on R. D. As he walked north along the railroad, he met black men going, singly or in groups of two or three, toward the village. These were, for the most part, men who composed the "outside crew." The outside crew—under the supervision of a white foreman—collected the village garbage, maintained the streets, and performed other unskilled labor outside the mill. Jim Henry was relieved to note the men greeted him in a manner that, while not exactly relaxed, was much less tense and hostile than the day before.

At R. D.'s the situation was much improved. Granny Foster predicted with some confidence that the worst had passed. R. D. was still running a fever, but he was awake more often, was eating well, and had more energy. Jim Henry decided he would not worry about R. D. or the black quarter today. He needed to be about other business.

* * *

The first thing the constable saw when he reached the village square was a young man nailing a notice to a tree near the company store. The young man finished, picked up the stack of papers at his feet, and moved on. Jim Henry saw the notice had been hurriedly typed. It read:

> **If any operative of Boiling Springs Mill, or any employee of the Boiling Springs Mill Company, molest or disturb any Negro or white person on any of the streets, roads or property of the company, they—with the families with whom they live—will be discharged, and asked to vacate any house owned by said company.**

Jim Henry knew two families were presently to be evicted. And he would be called on to enforce that eviction, so he decided to speak with Hames right away.

Forrest Hames was in his office and the constable was sent in immediately.

"Good mornin' Mr. Hames. I thought I'd check with you about the Hollis family and the Green family."

"Morning Constable. I told you yesterday, I want those families out of Boiling Springs. Zeno left word with the appropriate overseers. The employed family members were terminated immediately when they showed up for work."

"How long will they have to vacate their houses?"

"Today!"

Jim Henry looked distressed, "Mr. Hames, it's gonna fall to me to see that these folks leave. I don't wanna have to arrest nobody just 'cause they can't move out this minute." With a flash of inspiration he added, "It just don't seem it's Christian to not give 'em a little time."

Hames looked at Jim Henry. His temper rose. He knew he was being played, and he didn't like it at all. He also realized the constable had boxed him in.

"All right! They can have 'til sundown tomorrow. But not one minute longer. You see to it. You hear me constable?"

Jim Henry was already rising to leave.

"Yes sir," he said. "And that's right considerate Mr. Hames."

* * *

At the Hollis house there was anger, sadness, and fear. As Jim Henry was approaching the house, the younger children saw him and scampered inside. Shortly, Mrs. Hollis appeared on the porch. She was thin and stooped. At age forty two she looked all of sixty five.

"Jim Henry Tate? You come to throw us out?"

"It does seem that way, Miz Hollis. Though it ain't really me that's doin' it."

"But you're the law. You're gonna see that we leave."

He wanted to say it was George who was responsible, say that if the young man had not acted a fool she would not have to leave. Instead he said, "Yes ma'am. I reckon that's right. But right now I come to tell you that you have 'til tomorrow sundown."

The woman sat down heavily on the edge of the porch and began to sob. Jim Henry could think of nothing comforting to say. But it seemed to him rude to merely walk away. As he stood awkwardly wondering what to do, the small children came and stood peeking from just inside the door. He decided he would just sit on the edge of the porch while Mrs. Hollis had her cry. After a few minutes—minutes that seemed unusually long—the crying stopped.

"One of you young 'uns bring me a clean rag from the kitchen."

When a little girl came out with a small, worn cloth Mrs. Hollis took it, wiped her eyes, and blew her nose.

"Thank you darlin'. Don't you worry now. Mama's just tired. It's gonna be all right."

Was it time to leave? Jim Henry still felt odd about walking away. "They's lots of cotton mills around," he said.

Mrs. Hollis drew a deep breath, sighed and said, "I know they is. We'll just go up the road to Henrietta, or Caroleen. And I reckon we ain't no worst off now than we was 'fore we come here."

Hoping to distract her a bit from her immediate worries, Jim Henry asked, "Where're you folks from?"

"Oh, we come from the hills, up yonder north of Cherry Mountain."

Mrs. Hollis sat quietly for a bit looking first at the sky and then at the ground.

"I recollect when the recruiter come to the house. He talked powerful about good houses and making six dollars ever week, maybe as much as eight. The mister was taken with the idea. I said I wouldn't go. But, ... well, ... here I am."

The smallest child came and sat in her lap.

"This 'un was born here. They's another 'un we'll have to leave here when we go. The littlest one we brought from the hills took sick right after we got here. He's buried up yonder in the cemetery. I hate to go off and leave him."

After what he hoped was a decent interval, Jim Henry said, "I hate to ask, Miz Hollis, but is George around?"

She shook her head. "No, he ain't. I reckon that's another 'un I'll leave behind."

"Do you know where he is?"

"I don't. But I wouldn't tell you if I did, Jim Henry."

"I reckon that's right."

"He come tearin' in Saturday night, grabbed up what few clothes he had, and took off. I just wish he hadn't took up with that Green boy. George's really a good boy, but that Howard is a bad 'un."

Jim Henry looked at Mrs. Hollis in surprise. He wondered how she could be so blind. But a mother's love must be the blindest of all, he thought. He simply said, "Yes'm."

She sighed and looked at her hands.

"The mister's out tryin' to borrow a mule and wagon. We got two beds to move, along with some chairs and a table. Other'n that it's just some quilts, a few clothes, pots'n pans and such."

Finally the constable felt free to leave.

"All right Miz Hollis, I wish you well. Much as I'd rather not, I've gotta go on over to the Green's."

Jim Henry walked away down the dirt street. Just before a turn in the street, beyond which the house would not be visible, he looked back. Mrs. Hollis still sat with the child in her lap.

At the Green home things for Jim Henry were at once easier, and more difficult—easier because in short order he felt no sympathy for the family being evicted, more difficult because he came under immediate threat. When Jim Henry knocked at the door, Howard's father, Colin, came out, full of anger.

"I know why you're here, Constable Tate." He emphasized the word "constable" with a sneer. "It's because of some no count darkie. My boy was defendin' hisself—defendin' white folks if you ask me. Then here you come, doin' Forrest Hames' dirty work—against yore own race."

In spite of himself, Jim Henry backed up. Green, it appeared, was on the verge of attack.

"I ain't here to argue with you, Colin. I ain't happy I got to see that you move out neither. But yore boy brought this on you and his brothers. He went a-lookin' for trouble."

Green was beside himself.

"You git off my porch! Git back over to The Line with yore own kind! I'm proud of what my boy done. It's a shame the law in this little ole piss ant town won't protect white folks."

Jim Henry stepped off the porch. He hoped he had not moved so fast as to appear frightened. He knew that when dealing with people like Green one should never show any weakness.

"I'm goin'," he said, "but this ain't yore porch no more come sundown tomorrow. If you ain't out and gone by then I'll drag yer foul mouth and sorry ass to the lock up just as sure as God drove Adam out of Eden."

The constable turned and walked away, expecting to be attacked from behind at any minute. When the attack did not come, he breathed a sigh of relief.

* * *

Jim Henry entered the company store, thankful that his distasteful eviction duties were over, at least for today. Now he would find the information he needed to prove Rat Tail had killed Snag. He had intended to go directly to Harry Simmons, but the first person he saw upon entering the store was Rat Tail Summie. "Maybe," the constable muttered to himself, "I ought to see if I can rattle Rat Tail a mite."

Rat Tail greeted him with a smile.

"Mornin' Jim Henry. It's all over town that they was trouble on The Line. You've had a busy time of it, I reckon."

"Yep. But that's old business now. I'm back after who killed Snag. I hear you saw right much of ole Snag. Wuz you all kin?"

Rat Tail looked genuinely puzzled.

"Why, no, we weren't kin." Rat Tail shook his head, "I never thought I saw more of Snag than anybody else. Where'd you hear that, Jim Henry?"

"Oh, here and there. But ever body says the same. Says Snag was always comin' by to talk to you, hangin' round in menswear, and so on. Maybe you boys had some business together?"

Now Rat Tail did seem rattled. "Business? Me and Snag? Why, why no, we didn't have no business. I don't know what's got into you."

Jim Henry smiled. "Well, you know how this little ole place is. Ever body knows ever body's business. They know what ever body's doin'. If they've gone and got it wrong this time, it'll be right surprisin'."

"Well, whatever old busybodies you've been listenin' to, they surely got it wrong."

Jim Henry made a point of looking Rat Tail squarely in the eye. He smiled again and slowly said, "May be, maybe not. You take care, Rat Tail."

As he walked to the stairs leading to the manager's office, Jim Henry hummed a little tune. He was sure Rat Tail was the one. Rat Tail had to be the one. Too bad it was still his job to prove it. And too bad he had no idea how, or if, he could prove it.

Eula Morgan was not at her desk in Simmons' outer office, and the inner office door was closed. Jim Henry could hear conversation from the inner office, so he took a chair. Soon he looked around for something to read while he waited. Finding nothing, he sat for a short while longer and then began to pace. He was trying to decide whether to go away and return later or to knock on the manager's door when Eula emerged from the inner office with her steno pad in hand.

"Oh, hello Constable. I hope you haven't been waiting long."

"No, not long Miss Eula."

Simmons called through the open door, "Come on in, Jim Henry."

Harry Simmons came around his desk, took a seat and indicated the constable should take the seat opposite.

"What's on yer mind today?"

Jim Henry did not say that at that moment he was wondering, as did others in the village, exactly what the relation between Harry and Eula might be. Instead he said, "Two things. First, if I'm guessin' right, you won't be havin' no more theft. Second, I need to know ever thing they is to know about Rat Tail Summie."

"So it's Rat Tail?"

"I can't say that for sure. Let's just set that aside. Let's git on to that second thing. Tell me about Rat Tail."

Harry rubbed his chin.

"I'm not real sure I know anything you don't know. It seems he's scared of his wife. Good God! He ought to be. What a piece of work that woman is."

"Yeah, yeah, we all know that. But what else, Harry?"

"That's about all I know. Let's see. He's in the Red Men—but he's not a very good member. He misses about as many meetings as he attends. I know he's not in the Odd Fellows. And? Hmmm. He seems to attend church regular."

Jim Henry thought about these remarks for a moment or two. Then he said, "They must be more to him than that. Does he drink? Is he sneaky? Is he generous? Is what you've told me all they is to the man?"

After looking at the ceiling for a while Harry said, "Him and Eloise come here from over around Race Path Church."

"When was that?"

"They moved in, oh, let's see, must've been six year ago. Yeah, that's it; they come here in aught two. Before that he'd farmed a while. Farmed on land Eloise's folks owned, I believe. I don't know if he drinks. I don't know nothin' else about the man."

"Well hell! Who would know? Does he have any buddies? He run with anybody?"

Again Harry sat quietly for a time, and then said, "That's a good question. I'd never thought of it, but he don't seem to have no buddies. He don't hunt, far as I know. And he don't fish. The man must do somethin' with his spare time."

Jim Henry stood up. "He don't have no buddies? But Snag was around him a lot. 'Course, he denies that." Harry's small office did not allow for pacing. The constable sat back down.

Harry looked at Jim Henry and shook his head.

Jim Henry sighed, stood up again, and smiled.

"Okay. But Harry, you're into these fraternal things. When you

Red Men, or you Odd Fellows meet, who's the one who does a lot of talkin'? Who has all the local gossip?"

Harry grinned. "That'd be our good ole cotton buyer, Mr. Broadus White, who's in the Red Men."

"Then I need to be talkin' to Broadus. Thanks, Harry."

As he left, once again humming softly, Jim Henry said, "Good bye, Miss Eula. It's a right fine day, ain't it?"

* * *

Jim Henry did not see Broadus at the cotton gin. He did see a black driver sitting on an empty wagon near the gin. The constable walked over to the wagon.

"Mornin'. You seen the cotton buyer?"

"Um, oh, yes sir Cap'n. Mr. Broadus walk over to the cotton warehouse."

Broadus was in conversation with two black men at the cotton warehouse. When he saw Jim Henry, he held up a finger to signal he'd be free in a minute. The constable nodded.

Shortly the cotton buyer joined him.

"Jim Henry. You doin' constable business, or you just come to chat?"

"Both, I reckon. First off, I wanta say again that I'm obliged for your help night before last. I owe you."

"Well, a feller never knows when he might need a favor from the local law."

Both men chuckled.

"I'm tryin' to find out all I can about ole Rat Tail. I know he's in the Red Men with you, and I've been told you might know somethin' about him."

"Like what? Like he married a battle ax?"

"Not like that. I'm lookin' for somethin' that ain't as obvious as the nose on yer face. What sort of man is he anyway?"

Broadus scratched his head. Then he rubbed his chin. "That's hard to say. I've never had call to run around with him. Fact is, I don't see him around—outside of the company store, the church, or the Red Men. He don't seem to stand out. I guess he does his job well enough at the store."

"You say he don't stand out. Does he want to? For instance, does he want to do somethin' beside bein' a clerk?"

Broadus took a few steps in a tight circle. He rubbed his chin again and puffed.

"Whoo-whee. Since you ask, I think he's content just like he is. He won't accept any job in the church. And I don't know why he joined the Red Men. He comes to about half the meetings and when he's there he don't seem to join in. You know, he's just there. He don't enjoy hisself, or I don't think he does."

"That's funny. How long's he been a Red Man?"

"Not that long. He joined about six or eight months ago. Ever body made him welcome. But he's not one of the fellers, if you know what I mean."

"I guess I do."

Jim Henry stood waiting for Broadus to say more. But the cotton buyer offered nothing else.

"I don't think any of this'll help, but a feller never knows. Anything else you can think of?"

"I don't believe so. Like I say, Rat Tail don't stand out."

After another wait that produced only silence, Jim Henry said, "Who can you think of who might know more about Rat Tail?"

"You might try at the store."

"I just come from talkin' with Harry."

"No, I mean Byron or Hoyle, talk to them he works with."

Jim Henry slapped the cotton buyer on the shoulder, and said, "I'll do that Broadus. Thanks." He headed back to the company store.

Jim Henry spent the remainder of the morning talking with various employees of the company store. He then went home, found Joann gone, foraged for food, and returned to question store clerks all afternoon. He knew word of his inquiries would get back to Rat Tail, and he hoped that would prove an asset. He was certain Rat Tail was the killer, and because of that certainty, Jim Henry believed any pressure brought to bear on him would be advantageous—albeit in some vague, unknown way.

The tangible results of all this questioning were few, and seemed to add nothing to what was already known. Several hours of inquiry had produced three facts:

One: Everyone agreed that Rat Tail was a good employee and a pleasant enough associate. (Jim Henry could not see how that was helpful information.)

Two: Several commented that if they needed to step away from their post, to answer a call of nature, or what have you, Rat Tail was always eager to cover for them. (That would explain why the thefts, mainly in menswear, were sparsely scattered in other areas of the store. Otherwise it seemed useless knowledge.)

Three: Some few of the female clerks, and especially Rose the milliner, felt Rat Tail's interest in female customers, and employees, was more than might be considered appropriate for a married man. (Jim Henry thought this information unhelpful and, considering what he knew of Eloise, not surprising.)

* * *

At six o'clock that evening, Mae Belle Hudson left her spinning frame in the mill and walked up Main Street alongside several women with whom she worked. Coming from a family of five children, she had one older brother, one younger brother and two older sisters. As the youngest female in the family it was expected that Mae Belle would remain single, stay in the family home, and care for her parents as long as either of them lived. Her mother had died ten years before. She and her father, Roscoe, had moved to Boiling Springs four years previously.

Mae Belle knew her father would sit around outside the mill and chat for a while before coming home. For this evening he had no lodge meeting to attend—he was a Red Man—and he was not planning on going fishing. There was then no real need for Mae Belle to hurry home and start the evening meal. She thought she too would enjoy sitting outside the mill to hear the gossip, and perhaps contribute a bit. But that was not something women did—especially not young, attractive, single women. Mae Belle chuckled. She supposed she was still young, although at twenty three she was considered an old maid by most of the village.

After four blocks, Mae Belle said goodbye to her co-workers and turned toward the house one block east of Main Street that she shared with her father. This was a four room house and it was surprising it had been assigned to them by the mill company. Many cottages of that size held families of six or more.

Entering her home, Mae Belle saw a handbill lying on the seat of a rocker just inside the door. The handbill told of the revival that was to begin the next Sunday. There would be a service Sunday morning, and another Sunday evening. This would be followed by evening services throughout the following week. Mae Belle tore the flyer into strips. She would use these strips to start a fire in the kitchen stove.

Mae Belle opened the door to the stove's firebox, looked in and stood puzzled by what she saw. There was kindling carefully placed in the stove, with shredded paper underneath. How could that be? Neither she nor her father could have laid out the kindling before leaving for work, for the stove was still hot from her preparing breakfast. She called, "Dad?", but got no answer. Could he possibly have beaten her home, laid the kindling and then stepped out somewhere? That didn't seem likely. Did he come home during the day for some reason? Perhaps he'd been ill? After a moment or two she shrugged.

Mae Belle went to the back porch where a can of kerosene sat with an old empty salmon tin beside it. She poured kerosene into the can to a depth of about two inches, carried it in to the stove, and poured kerosene over the kindling. She struck a match and lit the kindling in the stove. The flames leapt up as she stood with the door open and watched. She thought she saw sparks within the flame. That was strange. Mae Belle bent down to look at the burning paper and wood. Then she began to close the door. It was the last thing she ever did.

* * *

Joann was in her garden gathering turnip greens when Jim Henry arrived home. He took a bottle of buttermilk from the ice box, poured himself a glass and sat on the back steps. He called to his wife, "You must have finished deliverin' the revival handbills."

"Yep, and you can see the clothes on the line. I've been working like a beaver."

"You ever see a beaver?"

"Nope, have you?"

"I saw one once, up around Brevard."

"You reckon beavers work as hard as folks say?"

"I expect. The one I saw had been bringin' down trees just like you hear about. Wonder why we don't have 'em around here?"

"I don't know."

Joann came and sat beside Jim Henry.

"How'd your day go? Did you make any progress?"

"I don't think I did. But we shouldn't ought to talk about it out here. What's for dinner?"

"Pinto beans, corn bread, and these greens. There's some ripe tomatoes. Why don't you pick them? I'll start fixing supper."

Later, as the couple sat inside waiting for the cornbread to bake, Jim Henry told Joann about his day.

"I can't find out a thing about Rat Tail. The man seems to have no life outside the store. He has no friends that I can find. He's a Red Man, but he don't attend meetin' but about half the time. He's a real loner."

"Hah! Look who's talking. You don't even belong to a lodge."

"But I have friends."

"Yeah? Well, you try to avoid every social event you can."

"But I go huntin' with Broadus. I shoot pool ever now and then. I even play a little poker with a few of the fellers—I hope the sheriff don't find out. He frowns on gamblin'."

"That's as may be. But church? Well, I really worry about you Law Man. You find more reasons to skip church!"

"I guess I do, but still, I like to think upholdin' the law is doin' good works. Surely that counts in my favor."

At that point there was a bang.

"What was that?"

"I don't know. It sounded somethin' like a gun shot, but then again it didn't. Maybe I ought to go out and see if they's somethin' wrong. How long 'til that cornbread's done?"

"Not long. You really think you should check? Somebody's always shooting at a snake, or a possum, or some such."

"But that didn't sound right. The way things've been the past few days .... hmmm .... I'll be back quick as I can."

With that, the constable picked up his gun belt and headed out the front door.

Jim Henry hurried east, the direction from which he believed the noise had come. As he crossed Main Street, he could hear people calling to one another. Everyone was hurrying toward Fourth Avenue. The constable turned down Fourth, and soon he saw a crowd gathering in front of the Hudson house. At the edge of the crowd he saw Scott Blanton from the livery stable.

"Scott, what's happened?"

"Seems they was some kinda explosion. I just got here."

A lady standing nearby chimed in, "Mae Belle had her stove blow up on her. They's some say she's dead."

Jim Henry grunted in response to this information; stoves didn't explode. He began to make his way toward the house.

"Y'all let me through. Excuse me. Ma'am, could I git through?"

Several men stood on the porch. They all nodded or spoke. Jim Henry looked around and asked, "Is Roscoe here?"

There were several murmurs.

"No." "Don't know where he is." "Ain't seen him."

"Well, who's with Mae Belle?"

"They's two neighbor women with her in the kitchen."

Jim Henry went inside. Soot covered every flat surface and hung from curtains. In the kitchen, Mae Belle lay on the floor with her feet toward the iron stove. She was covered with soot and her clothing was singed. Blood had run from her ears and nose, and a wooden splinter had pierced her cheek.

One woman was kneeling beside Mae Belle. The other sat beside her in one of the kitchen chairs. They both looked at Jim Henry and shook their heads.

"Dr. Callahan's been sent for, but it ain't no use."

Jim Henry looked around the small room. As in most of the mill houses, there was a small iron woodstove, a table with several chairs, and a kitchen cabinet. The stove sat in a corner of the room. To the left of the stove was a door leading to a small porch. To the right of the stove was a window with several broken panes. All the stove's cast iron eyes (lids from the stove's "burners") had been blown off. The stove was cracked in several places and the fire box door hung by a single hinge.

"Ladies, what you all reckon happened here?"

The two women looked at each other. One replied, "The stove blowed up."

"But stoves don't blow up. Kerosene cans blow up. Where's the kerosene can?"

Jim Henry looked around the kitchen. An empty salmon tin was in the corner of the room opposite the stove, but there was no kerosene can. He then went out to the back porch.

On the porch sat a can of kerosene. Something was not right here. As the constable stood looking at the can, he heard one of the women call to him. "Constable, here's Dr. Callahan."

Back in the kitchen the doctor was shooing the women away.

"Move back now. In fact, maybe you ladies could go in the other room. There's very little space in here."

Jim Henry stood at the door and watched as the doctor painfully lowered himself to a kneeling position beside Mae Belle.

"Yore knees hurtin' again Callie?"

"Hell yes; they complain every time I get up or sit down. They say it's downhill after forty; after seventy it's, well I don't know what it is, but it's not real good."

Though he knew it was futile, the doctor felt for a pulse at Mae Belle's wrist, and then again at her neck. He looked up at the constable.

"She's dead, Jim Henry."

"I figured as much, Callie. How you reckon this happened?"

"I don't rightly know, Jim Henry."

At that moment a commotion began in the yard. It quickly moved into the house. Mae Belle's father had arrived.

Roscoe Hudson, a bear of a man, burst into the kitchen.

"What in hell's happened here? What's wrong with Mae Belle? Is she gonna be all right?"

Jim Henry placed a hand on Roscoe's arm. The man knocked it away and turned on Jim Henry with a snarl.

"Keep yore hands off me. What're you doing here? Who sent for the law?"

The constable backed off a step or two. "Roscoe, calm down now. I'm here to help if I can, to figure out what happened. All we know is Mae Belle's gone."

Roscoe looked wildly about the kitchen, then at the doctor.

"She ain't dead, doctor! She ain't. She ain't ... she ain't."

Dr. Callahan slowly nodded. "Yes Roscoe, she's gone. I wish it wasn't so, but it is."

Hudson threw one of the kitchen chairs against the wall. He turned and stomped for a bit and then sat down heavily in one of the remaining chairs. Tears began to roll down his cheeks and he angrily brushed them away. He took out a large red and grey handkerchief and loudly blew his nose. The tears started again and this time Roscoe bent forward holding his stomach. His body shook as he choked back sob after sob, determined to keep quiet.

Dr. Callahan, unable to remain kneeling any longer asked Jim Henry to help him stand. Then he said, "I can't do much on the floor with my knees half killing me. If you men would, step out and ask the two ladies to come back in. I'd like to move Mae Belle onto one of the beds so I can examine her. I need to see if I can tell whether there was something other than the blast killed her."

Roscoe immediately snarled, "I ain't leavin'."

The doctor rubbed his face.

"Roscoe, don't you want to allow Mae Belle some dignity? Even if she is dead, do you really think she'd want you lookin' on while I examine her?"

"Then don't examine her. It won't do no good. She's dead. God! Damn! It!

Jim Henry spoke up.

"Roscoe, they's somethin' that ain't right here. They was some sort of explosion—we don't know what kind. We don't know what else might've happened, if anything. You want us to find all we can about Mae Belle's death, don't you?"

Roscoe just stared at his daughter's body. Jim Henry tried again.

"Roscoe, let's me and you go out back, away from that crowd in the front. Let's let Callie do his job. I don't reckon none of us can help Mae Belle right now. But I believe they's been some devilment here. We need to know all we can. You need to let the doctor do his job. Maybe he can help me do mine."

Slowly Roscoe dried his eyes, blew his nose again, rose and walked past Jim Henry onto the back porch. Jim Henry opened the door into the front room, called the women in, and joined Roscoe on the porch.

After trying to make conversation for a few minutes, Jim Henry asked if Roscoe would rather be alone.

"Yeah Jim Henry, I reckon I would. I ain't in the mood for talk. I'm mad as hell, and broke all up, and … and, I just want to tear somethin' up—or tear somebody up."

"Then I'll be about my business."

With that, the constable went around the house to the front yard.

Scanning the crowd for people who lived close to Roscoe and Mae Belle, Jim Henry spotted Mrs. Hightower, an elderly widow who lived with her daughter and son-in-law across the street and just opposite the Hudson house. Mrs. Hightower spent warm weather on her daughter's front porch and cold weather at the window of the front room. Very little, if anything, that happened nearby escaped Mrs. Hightower's notice. The constable made his way to her side.

"Terrible thing, Miz Hightower."

"Yes, constable, it shore is. I ain't never seen a thing just like it."

"You notice anything unusual around the Hudson house today?"

Suddenly the old lady seemed to take a short step backward, a very unstable step. Jim Henry, frightened she was about to fall, took her elbow.

"Miz Hightower, let me walk you back to yore porch. You can set down there and we can talk a while. I expect you can help me figure out what happened here."

Once Mrs. Hightower was settled in a rocker, Jim Henry pulled a straight chair up and sat looking at the people milling in the Hudson's yard.

"You spend a lot of time on this porch don't you, Miz Hightower?"

"Well, I reckon I do. With the young folks at work and the grandchildren runnin' all over the mill hill, I set out here and watch folks come and go—all by myself. Now and then a body'll stop in and chat for a spell. But mostly folks don't have no time for a wore out old widder woman like me."

Jim Henry thought comments of that sort likely ensured people would choose to avoid stopping in to "chat for a spell." He also thought Mrs. Hightower sounded remarkably like his own mother. Jim Henry was an only child. His mother was widowed and lived alone in Marion, close to forty miles away. He knew some change in her living arrangements needed to be made, and made soon. He also knew he didn't want to think about that now. There were other, pressing things to think about. Actually, Jim Henry was relieved there were other things to think about, but that relief also came accompanied by feelings of guilt. He sighed and asked, "How about today, Miz Hightower? Were you out here today?"

"Right much of the day, yes. I know it's wash day, but that there's just got beyond me. Even if I could wash clothes I couldn't wring 'em out, nor hang 'em to dry. They get wet, they're just too heavy for me."

"Were you out when Mae Belle come home?"

"Oh yes, I seen her come walkin' down from Main Street like always. She went directly into the house—didn't even look over this way. I don't think Mae Belle felt very friendly toward me. I don't know why."

"Was anybody with her when she come home?"

"Oh no! She was by herself. Pore thing, I don't think she has many friends—or *had* many friends, I should say."

"How long was it after she went in the house before the explosion?"

"I reckon it couldn't have been more'n three or four minutes. She must've gone straight to light her stove."

"Was they anybody around her house before Mae Belle come home?"

"No, no, I don't believe they was. And I reckon I was here for about a hour before she come in."

Jim Henry tipped his chair back. Joann was constantly telling him not to do that, for fear he'd break the chair legs. But it was a habit he'd not been able to rid himself of.

"What do you reckon happened to Mae Belle over there?"

"I don't rightly know, constable. I once saw a kerosene can

explode on a woman—well, I saw her after the explosion. She come runnin' outer her house all aflame. But this weren't like that at all."

"Something exploded, that's for sure. But I agree it weren't the kerosene can."

As Jim Henry sat wondering what he should ask next, he saw Amos Scruggs arrive. Amos was busier than usual, he thought. Bodies were coming at the rate of one a week. And they were coming in a way it was his job to stop. He shook his head; he'd sure be hearing from Forrest Hames pretty soon.

"You said Mae Belle seemed to have few friends. Did she have any enemies you know of, Miz. Hightower?"

"No, I don't think so. She was a nice, quiet, hardworking girl. Took good care of her pa."

Jim Henry sat quietly, hoping the old lady would add more. He felt there had to be something more to be said about Mae Belle. But nothing was forthcoming. He stood and said, "Well I thank you Miz. Hightower. If you remember anything that happened at the Hudson's today—anything that seemed like it was outta the ordinary—please let me know."

Back in the yard of the Hudson house, Jim Henry saw the entire Hunnicutt family—mother, father, and four children—standing together near the porch. The Hunnicutt house was just west of the Hudson house. He approached the father, Jeff.

"Jeff, were you here when this blast went off?"

"No, I just got here a minute or so ago. Minnie was here though."

"I see. Miz Hunnicutt, did you see Mae Belle come home?"

"No, I guess I must've got home just ahead of her."

"Tell me what you remember about the explosion."

"Well, I went in the house and looked for the young 'uns. Turns out they was all in back of the house. Then, ... let's see, ... I saw this flyer about the revival laying on our bed in the front room. I set on the edge of the bed and read that. I was about to lay back on the bed and rest a minute when I heard this terrible boom. 'Course I run out to see what happened."

"Did you see anybody around the Hudson house when you went out?"

"Well, no, not right away. But soon the neighbors commenced to come out and head that way, toward the Hudson house. I was right conflicted about what to do. I knowed somethin' terrible had happened. I thought Mae Belle was shorely hurt. But I, well, I don't know, I just stood there dreadin' goin' over. And, well, I never did go in. I still ain't seen Mae Belle. Is it true she's dead?"

"Yes ma'am, it is."

"A terrible thing. What you reckon caused that blast?"

"I wish I knew. I can't think what could've been around that stove that would've caused it to blow up."

After a moment or two, Jim Henry said, "Well, I thank you. Guess I'd best talk to some other folks and see what I can learn."

* * *

Joann was just lighting a lamp when Jim Henry came in. She said, "I heard from the folks next door what happened. I figured I couldn't help out any over there, and the crowd was probably big enough."

"You was right. Nobody could help, and they was a bunch over there."

"Sit down. I'll get you some food. I ate while it was hot."

As she dished food onto a plate, Joann asked, "Did you find out what caused the explosion? I guess it was an accident of some sort?"

"If it was, it was the damnedest accident I ever heard tell of. I don't know what happened, but it don't seem right. They's some devilment here."

Jim Henry ate in silence for a time.

"I'm thinkin' I ought to give up being constable and get me a job in the mill."

"Whatever do you mean?"

"Well, people getting' shot, cut up, blowed up, and what am I doin' about it? Not one hell of a lot. I just don't know, Joann."

Joann smiled. She shook her head.

"You know you'd be miserable in that mill. Come on! You're the Law Man."

Jim Henry laughed.

"I don't reckon I'd like bein' a linthead. You got that right."

"Well, just tell me what you know about Mae Belle getting blown up. I'll get my pencil and paper."

"That's about it. She got blowed up. I talked to lots of folks and all I know is she got blowed up." Jim Henry ate for a bit. "She come home; she must've gone straight to light a fire in the stove, and somehow somethin' in the stove blowed up. 'Course the first thing you think of is kerosene. But the kerosene can was outside, and it weren't damaged."

"Then you think somebody put something in her stove?"

"I think that's got to be it."

Joann wrote for a while on her note pad.

"You told me anything I can't report?"

"Don't say somebody put somethin' in the stove. Just say they was an explosion."

"I kind of figured that." Joann wrote for a while, then she asked, "What about Mae Belle's dad, Roscoe?"

"He's right broke up, and mad as hell. He's gonna stay with one of his Red Man buddies tonight. Soot's thick all over that house. I expect he'll want to move. He can probably have either the Greene house or the Hollis house. They've got to be gone by tomorrow evenin'."

Joann made some notes. "I hate to do it, but I should report on those families being put out of the company houses too. It is news."

"Well, that's true. And it's all a part of that ruckus on The Line. No reason I can see why you ought not."

"This week the paper will have the biggest news about Boiling Springs I bet there's ever been."

Jim Henry refilled his plate. "Big news, bad news."

Joann wrote some more. Then she put her pad aside. After a moment she said, "Roscoe's gonna miss having Mae Belle wash and iron and cook for him. He'll find out pretty quick how easy he's had it—and how tough Mae Belle had it."

Jim Henry merely grunted in reply.

"So all that gets is a grunt? You don't know how good you've got it either, Jim Henry Tate."

The constable grunted again and Joann punched him on the shoulder.

"Well then, so much for that. How about Mae Belle's burying?"

Jim Henry held up a finger to indicate that he couldn't speak just then. He chewed vigorously and visibly, swallowed, and said, "Since the house is in such a mess she's gonna be put in the town hall. They's two ladies'll dress her and help Amos git her laid out. I guess they'll be a funeral service in the church, but I don't know if it'll be tomorrow or Wednesday. That's all up in the air."

"Well, tomorrow I can add the details about her funeral. I'll forget about it 'til tomorrow. Why don't you do the same?"

"God, I'd like to! Wish I could put all this mess away as easy as you puttin' down yore pencil and paper."

"Maybe you can. Finish your supper and we'll see."

DAY NINE

Jim Henry woke with a start. He was gripped by a general, amorphous unease. He sat up in bed. He looked in vain for Joann, and heard her in the kitchen. Then he remembered. Mae Belle was dead. Not just dead, but certainly murdered. He fell back onto his pillow. His job now was to find two murderers—but how?

Joann appeared at the bedroom door.

"Thought I heard you. I was about to come see if you were still breathing. It's seven already."

Jim Henry groaned. "I ought to just stay in bed. I really don't know what I'm gonna do today." He sighed, "I think I've got my eye on who killed ole Snag, and then this happens. Who'd want to kill Mae Belle?"

Joann sat on the bed and rubbed Jim Henry's chest. "Don't know." Then after a moment she said, "You spent yesterday trying to learn all you could about Rat Tail. Maybe today you ought to find all you can about Mae Belle."

Jim Henry sighed again, swung his legs off the bed, and sat up.

"Yeah, I suppose that's the thing to do." He puffed. "What is it Broadus says? If you're gonna get goin' you've gotta get goin'. Guess I better get goin'."

"That's it Law Man! Now do what you gotta do before breakfast, and come eat. I've added water to the grits more times than I can count keeping them warm for you."

"I'm on my way. Is they any livermush?"

After breakfast the constable went straight to the mill, and up to the spinning room on the top floor. Here young women watched over machines called spinning frames. These were large machines that took loose ropes of cotton fiber, called roving, thinned and twisted them to create yarn, and wound the yarn onto bobbins. It was not uncommon to find only two adult males in a spinning room, a mechanic who repaired the spinning machinery, and a supervisor. Jim Henry had come to talk with Mae Belle's cohorts. And, he had to admit, he had come to hide from Forrest Hames. Hames was sure to be looking for him.

Upon entering the spinning room, Jim Henry saw a notice tacked to one of the beams supporting the mill's roof. This announced that Mae Belle Hudson's funeral would be held in the Baptist church at seven that evening, with burial following immediately.

After reading the notice, Jim Henry spotted Nina Cash standing at the end of her frame. The spinning frame was shut down and two young doffing boys were busy replacing full bobbins with empty ones. The woman would not be idle for long, so Jim Henry hurried to her side.

"Mornin' Nina. I'd be grateful if I could talk to you a minute."

"Hey, Jim Henry. You better talk fast, or you're gonna have to foller me around and let me yell over my shoulder."

"Yeah, I know. I expect you've heard about Mae Belle?"

"I have. Terrible thing."

"It is. And, well, it looks kinda like they was somethin' done to her stove. And that got her killed."

"That's what folks is sayin'."

"Would you know anybody who'd have it in for her?"

"No, I don't reckon so. Uh ... uh ... come on Jim Henry. I've gotta start my frame back up."

Jim Henry walked along, staying behind Nina and just to her left.

"Well, if you don't know of any enemies, who was her friends?"

"Oh, I think all of us was her friends." Nina stopped, then

turned and faced the constable. "But when you get right down to it, they was nobody she was all that close to."

"So you yourself didn't see her 'cept here at the mill?"

The spinner turned back to her frame and said, "Come on, Jim Henry. We had pretty near nothin' in common."

"Yeah, I reckon that's right. You're already a married woman and she was already an old maid, even though you're what, about half her age?"

"I'm not that young, and she weren't that old. She was about five year older'n me though."

"She mighta been an old maid, but she sure was a pretty woman. Didn't she have no men friends?"

"She never spoke about no boyfriend. I never saw her with nobody. But, well, I might shouldn't say this, but Vernon sure was after her."

Jim Henry thought this interesting information. Vernon Ladshaw was the overseer in the spinning room, and as such, the immediate superior to all the women tending frames.

Nina put her hand to her lips. "I talk way yonder too much. Don't you let on to nobody I told you."

"I won't Nina. But I'm obliged to you, and I'll get outta yer way now."

Jim Henry began looking for Vernon, but the overseer was nowhere to be found. So he approached another spinner.

"Hello, Virginia. Can you talk with me while you work?"

"Why not? I guess you wanna talk about Mae Belle?"

"I do. It might be somebody fixed her stove up so as it killed her. You have any idea who'd do that?"

"Good Lord no! I don't associate with folks that'd kill somebody."

"Well, who was Mae Belle's friends? Who'd know most about her?"

"Mae Belle didn't seem to have no real friends. Bless her heart, all she done was work in this mill and look after her daddy."

"So you didn't see her outside the mill?"

"I saw her at church. But that's all."

"How about men? Was she seein' anybody?"

"Now, Jim Henry. I can tell you right off, they wasn't nothin' between her and Vernon."

"Oh! Why would you say that? Is they somethin' I should know about her and Vernon?"

"Nothin' 'cept Vernon thought since Mae Belle was older, and single, she'd be wantin' to fall in bed with 'im. That Vernon! Like my mama said, you men think with yore little head, not the one on yore shoulders."

Jim Henry laughed. "Well, thanks a lot for that Virginia ... I guess."

"You know it's so. No need for me to pussyfoot around about it."

"So you're tellin' me she weren't seein' nobody?"

"That's right. I'm thinkin' she wasn't interested in any men 'round here. She sure as tootin' weren't interested in Vernon, that alley cat!"

"Speak of the devil! I see he just walked in. Thanks, Virginia. I won't mention to Vernon yer opinion of him."

The spinner merely snorted and moved away.

Vernon Ladshaw's office was a nine by eleven area partitioned off in the northeast corner of the spinning room. The office had no door, and the walls, such as they were, did not reach the ceiling. The walls were wood only from the floor to a height of about four feet; from there glass rose another three feet.

Ladshaw was a tall thin man with a pencil line mustache and an oily comb-over with a part that started only a few inches above his ear. He wore a dark brown suit with light brown shirt, dark brown tie and a pale yellow vest. The head spinner was seated behind his desk, and there was no other chair in the room. Clearly this arrangement was meant to let any visitor know their lack of status relative to Vernon Ladshaw. Jim Henry entered and stood smiling at the head spinner.

Ladshaw looked up from the forms on his desk.

"What's that smirk on yore face, Jim Henry?"

"That's not a smirk. I was just thinkin' how funny it must be when Forrest Hames comes by. Do you let him set behind the desk while you stand?"

"I reckon that's none of yore business. What're you doin' in my spinnin' room anyway?"

"I'm tryin' to learn if anybody had it in for Mae Belle."

Ladshaw leaned back in his chair. "I don't know, but I bet nobody had it *in* Mae Belle, if you know what I mean."

"That's real helpful Vernon, and classy too. I guess that means she turned you down, huh?"

"Who says she did? I never went after that ole maid. I don't think she even liked men. You know they is women like that."

"So you don't know of any man she mightta been seein'?"

"Oh hell no! Like I said. She was a cold one for sure."

"How about here at work? She git along with ever body?"

"She shore did. I don't keep people in my department if they can't git along. I don't allow no fussin' and goin' on. People can't work that a-way. And my people work. They do good work."

"I'll let Hames know that the next time he asks me how things're goin' in the spinnin' room."

"They's no need to smart mouth me, Jim Henry. Why don't you just go on and leave me alone anyway. Some folks have to work for a livin' you know."

"Oh yeah?" Jim Henry shook his head. "I do thank you Vernon, for all your help—I reckon. I'll see you around."

Jim Henry spent the better part of another hour talking with spinners. But he learned nothing further of any interest. He was going down stairs to exit the mill, when he suddenly realized that though he dreaded a meeting with him, Forrest Hames could actually have useful information. With a sigh, he headed for the old man's office.

Jim Henry had not finished asking Hames' secretary if he was in before Hames bellowed, "Constable! Why have you let my town turn into a little Chicago?"

Jim Henry walked through to Forrest's office.

"I don't rightly know what you're talkin' about Mr. Hames."

"Yes you do! There are people getting killed every week! Why, I bet for our size we're having even more murders than they have in Chicago."

"Yes sir, maybe for the last couple of weeks that might be true. But now, we're not real sure Mae Belle was murdered, are we?"

"Thunderation Constable! Everybody in the whole village thinks she was. Are you telling me her death was an accident?"

"No sir, I can't tell you that. And I do think somebody put somethin' in her stove. I think that, but I don't know it."

"Well, what's your plan Constable Tate?"

"My plan is to find out who put somethin' in Mae Belle's stove—if somebody did—and arrest 'em. I also plan to find who killed Snag and arrest them."

Hames began to say something, but Jim Henry held his hand up with palm toward the old man.

"Please! Let me finish. I came in here because you might be able to help me."

Hames again began to speak, hesitated, grunted, threw up his hands and leaned back in his chair.

Inwardly, Jim Henry breathed a sigh of relief. "Okay, here's how you can help. Is they anything used in the mill that could cause a stove to blow up like Mae Belle's did?"

Hames sat silent for so long Jim Henry thought he was not going to answer. But finally he said, "The only things we use, except cotton, are starch and indigo. I know starch dust can explode if there's a flame—or even a spark of some sort. But a pile of starch in a stove wouldn't explode. You'd have to have the air inside the stove full of starch dust."

"I don't see how that could happen. If somebody blew starch dust into Mae Belle's stove, it'd settle out pretty quick."

"That's so. Now as to indigo, I suppose in dry powder form it would act just like starch."

"And for the same reason as starch, it couldn't have been what caused Mae Belle's death."

"That's got to be right. And I really can't see how anybody could create enough fine cotton dust—anywhere outside the mill—to cause an explosion. So no, I believe there's nothing we use in the mill that could be used to cause a stove to explode."

Both men sat quietly for a minute or so. Then Jim Henry asked, "What about dynamite? It could be somebody hid a stick of dynamite in Mae Belle's stove. That would do the trick."

"Well certainly. That's what dynamite's for—to blow things up."

"So, how about dynamite? Is they any of it out where folks could git hold of it?"

"Hmmm. I expect lots of farmers might have some dynamite. They'd use it for blasting out tree stumps, and so on. We don't sell any in the store, but they could buy it other places not too far away."

"How 'bout 'round the mill? Is they any dynamite stored in the mill?"

Again Hames sat quietly for a considerable time. "I don't really know. There might be some dynamite left over from clearing right of way for the railroad. It wouldn't be stored in the mill though. If there's any left it ought to be in the train shed."

"So anybody could git to it? That shed's never locked. Ain't that right?"

"Oh no, that's not right! The shed's not locked in daytime, but it is locked at night.

"All right then. Who'd know for sure if they's any dynamite in the train shed?"

"Let me see. I believe Rush Hamrick would know. He's the outside foreman."

Again both men sat in silence for a time. Finally Jim Henry got to his feet.

"Thanks Mr. Hames. I think I better go talk to Rush."

As the constable was leaving, Hames called, "See that those two families are gone today! And about Zebulon Wiley's death—you have two days."

* * *

It was almost an hour before the constable was able to find anyone who knew the whereabouts of Rush Hamrick. Then the information was disappointing. Rush had gone to Gaffney about some pipe fittings and would likely not return before evening.

What should he do now? Surely food would help him think—or at least not hinder his thinking. Jim Henry headed for home.

When he arrived, there was a note on the kitchen table. Joann had gone to Henrietta to deliver her news article about the trouble on The Line, the explosion, and Mae Belle's death. Jim Henry was on the back porch taking a bottle of butter milk from the ice box when he heard his wife come in the front.

"I assume that's my wayward wife. I'm out back here trying to find something to eat."

"You poor man! I can tell just by looking that you're about to starve."

"You can joke if you want to, but I'm about growed together in the middle."

Joann laughed. "Well, get some eggs while you're out there and bring the butter. I'll punch up the fire and we'll have eggs, cheese, tomatoes and cold biscuits."

Later as the couple ate, Jim Henry told Joann of his unproductive morning. Joann listened without comment until it seemed the constable had finished, then she asked, "Has it occurred to you how much alike the lives of Rat Tail and Mae Belle seem?"

"I reckon not. What do you mean?"

"Well, just look at their situations—before Mae Belle died, of course. In both cases any sort of social life just doesn't exist. By all reports neither had any real friendships. Mae Belle was single and Rat

Tail's married, of course. But I'm not the only one around who wonders what kind of a marriage he has. It just might be like no marriage at all."

Jim Henry laughed. "Why don't you just say that neither one of 'em was gittin' any?"

"Because proper women don't talk that way. But I see you understand what I was saying."

"Which brings to mind..."

"Forget it. I've got gardening to do and ironing as well."

"People are gonna wonder what kinda marriage we have."

"Well let 'em wonder."

After a moment or two, Joann said, "Since Rush has gone to Gaffney, you've told me what you're not going to be doing this afternoon. But what do you think you *are* going to be doing?"

"Ummm. I don't rightly know. I'm pretty well stumped. I guess for a while I'm gonna set out on the front porch in the shade and think."

"I've got a better idea. Why don't you think while you help me in the garden?"

* * *

As Jim Henry pulled weeds from around the tomatoes and beans he went over and over the little he knew about Mae Belle's death. He straightened his back, groaned and said, "How could we have another murder just right after Snag's in such a little bitty ole town? It just don't seem right."

Joann stopped her hoeing and leaned on the hoe. "I've been thinking about that. Maybe the two deaths are not completely separate happenings."

"But what connection could they be between Snag and Mae Belle?"

Joann nodded toward the yard of their neighbor to the east. The family's five year old daughter stood at the edge of the garden looking their way.

"We better not talk about this anymore right here."

"Good morning, Martha Ann."

The young girl answered, "It's not morning."

"Oh, well, that's right. Good afternoon Martha Ann."

Martha Ann turned and ran away.

* * *

Gardening finished, Jim Henry sat and watched Joanne iron. They discussed Mae Belle and Snag for a time. Then Jim Henry said, "Well, as Broadus says...."

"I know, I know, 'this ain't gettin' the baby no new shoes.' Does Broadus really say all these things or do you just make them up?"

"Of course he says these things."

"I bet!"

"Sure enough." The constable stood up. "Anyway, I reckon I can at least check to see that the Hollis and Green families have moved out. Maybe some idea will jump out and grab me while I'm doin' that."

"Does Broadus say things like 'Some idea will jump out and grab me,' really?"

"I don't know about that one. That may be from somebody else; it might even be mine."

Jim Henry strapped on his revolver. Joann grimaced.

"You can't never tell Joann. GeeHaw might have slipped back around. And Green is a right mean 'un. I think he'd like nothin' better'n to lay me out for good."

The constable was already off the porch when he turned, came back inside, gave Joann a kiss on the cheek and said, "I might've just figured somethin' out. Well, part way anyhow. We need to go to Mae Belle's buryin' this evening. And I need to talk to a beautiful woman—other than you, of course."

"Just you go on; I'm not real worried. There's no woman but me could put up with you."

* * *

At the Hollis house no one answered Jim Henry's knock. He went inside and walked through the house. Not only was it completely empty, but the floors appeared to have been scrubbed. The constable stood and shook his head. How could such a family have produced such a totally worthless son as George? Was GeeHaw responsible for Snag's death? And where were they anyway? In South Carolina as everyone suspected? Best to check.

No one was home in the house to the right, and there were only two children in the house to the left. Jim Henry walked across the street to the home facing the vacated Hollis home. A young woman answered his knock. She had a nursing child held to her breast and was in the process of draping a diaper over her shoulder and the child.

"Hey Mavis. Sorry to bother you. Picked a bad time, I guess."

"That's all right Jim Henry. What is it?"

"I just wanted to see if you had noticed George around 'fore the Hollis folks left."

"No. But I think they was lookin' for him to show up."

"I expect they was. Not surprised he didn't though. Sorry to have bothered you. How's the young 'un doin'?"

"Oh, she's fine. Eats like a little pig. She's three months tomorrow."

As he stepped off the porch the young mother said, "They was a good family. It's a shame they got run off."

The Green house was also empty, but it bore no other resemblance to the Hollis house. There was paper trash and empty tin cans in the kitchen. The floors appeared not to have been swept in months. In the back bedroom, there was even a torn and stained sheet thrown into a corner. Jim Henry grunted. If Roscoe Hudson was given the choice he would not choose this house. No one would. It needed a week of cleaning.

Like all houses in the village, the Green house was built on piers. Since this house sat on a steep hill, the piers in back of the house were six to eight feet tall. Jim Henry decided he would walk around to the back of the house and see what was underneath.

Judging by the empty jars underneath the house it was clear that Howard, or Colin, or the whole family, had been heavy consumers of 'shine. Perhaps they had also been involved in selling it. In any event, the constable thought, good riddance!

Jim Henry heard someone walking overhead in the house. Thinking it might be Haw come back, he sprinted around the house, stopped at the front door and drew his revolver. As he stepped inside, a middle aged lady turned, saw him, and let out a yelp.

"Jim Henry Tate, what are you doin'? You scared me half to death. Put that gun away. Do I look like some criminal? My Lord!"

Jim Henry blushed. "I'm right sorry Miz Moore. I was under the house and heard you walkin' around. I thought it might be Howard up here."

"Well, he ain't here. I was just deliverin' the rest of my revival flyers, and thought I'd look in. Ain't this place a mess? How can folks live like this? I swear, hogs probably live better. My Lord!"

"Yes'm, it sure is a mess."

Mention of revival flyers brought the constable's mind back to Mae Belle Hudson's death.

"Miz Moore, you mentioned them flyers. Did you deliver down by the Hudson's house yesterday? I'm lookin' for anybody who might've seen somethin' strange around there."

"My Lord! Weren't that terrible? That pore woman."

"Yes'm, it was awful. Was you by there yesterday?"

"No, that section weren't mine. I don't know for sure who was supposed to deliver there. It might have been Eloise."

"Eloise Summie?"

"Yes, My Lord! Don't that woman put on airs? I feel right sorry for ole Rat Tail—or I should say Ralph. Eloise turns blue ever time somebody calls him Rat Tail. I guess I ought to feel sorry for her too. She ain't no happy woman. I don't know what these younger women want. The Summies are a lot better off than some folks—better off than me and Jake has ever been. But God bless 'im, Jake's a good man, and a hard worker. Why ain't Eloise happy? She ought to be."

Jim Henry, unable to think of any response, merely said, "Yes'm."

"Well, I got to go Jim Henry. My Lord! This place is a mess. I wouldn't have my dogs in a place like this. You talk to Eloise. I think she will be the one delivered to the Hudsons. I hear Mae Belle's buryin' is tonight. I hope they's a good crowd. She was a nice person—never said a bad word about nobody."

"Yes'm."

"Got to go Jim Henry. I can't stand and talk all day."

"Yes'm."

And with that Mrs. Moore took her leave. Jim Henry felt just a bit dazed. He smiled. "My Lord!"

Jim Henry decided to put GeeHaw and their unfortunate families out of his mind. He thought about a connection between the deaths of Snag and Mae Belle. Could there be one? What could that connection be? He made for the company store and that beautiful woman he'd told Joann about. As he had expected, the milliner was still at her post.

"Afternoon, Miss Rose. Glad I caught you before you left. I need a minute of yore time."

"Good afternoon constable. I do declare I believe you are workin' up your courage to buy your lovely wife a new hat."

"No ma'am. That ain't so. But I want to ask you if you ever saw Mae Belle in here."

"Mae Belle Hudson? That poor woman! Do you mean recently?"

"Well, recently, or not so recently. You did notice that Snag was in and out right often. I just wondered about Mae Belle."

The milliner stood with her hand to her cheek.

"You know, I don't recall I ever saw her in here. I'd see her once in a while at church, and on the street of an evening or Saturday afternoon. But in the store? No, I don't believe so. Is that important?"

Jim Henry stood for a moment looking at nothing in particular. "I don't rightly know Miss Rose."

The constable left the store dejected. He still believed there was a connection between Snag's death and that of Mae Belle. But what *exactly* was that connection? And what about proof? He saw none.

* * *

At Mae Belle's funeral service, Joann moved them well toward the front of the church before Jim Henry could stop her. For his purposes he wanted to be further back, so he could see who was there. He squirmed around in his seat and looked over the audience. The turnout was modest. There were the older women who could be depended upon to be in church any time its doors were open. Several women from the spinning room were there, as was a scattering of the supervisory staff from the mill. Jim Henry noticed that Vernon Ladshaw was absent, and didn't know exactly what to make of that. Was Ladshaw so angry at being rebuffed? If so, how much more angry might he have been? Angry enough to hide dynamite in her stove? He didn't think so, and yet....

After some time, the constable looked over the audience again and saw Rat Tail without Eloise. Interesting, he thought. Then he saw Broadus and Harry. Apparently the Red Men were supporting their lodge brother Roscoe.

The funeral began, and shortly the pastor's comments left Jim Henry wondering if the Rev. Tarleton had known Mae Belle at all. But, he thought, an experienced clergyman probably need not know the person whose funeral he was to conduct. A short time with a family member no doubt gave bits of information that could be inserted into a format that had been used many, many times. This thought led the constable to wonder who, if anyone, had really known Mae Belle?

Had Mae Belle been satisfied with her life? Or had restrictive tradition created for her a prison without bars? In his mind's eye he saw cotton yarn tying Mae Belle to her spinning frame. Then he seemed to see more threads tying her to her father. Suddenly she became black! But no, that wasn't Mae Belle, it was LuElla. There he stood again on The Line with LuElla asking, "Can you reckon what it's like to be colored in this little ole town?" Certainly, vile tradition had built a prison around LuElla.

Jim Henry flinched as Joann's elbow poked in his ribs. He looked at her with his most sheepish grin. He had drifted off. He certainly hoped he had not snored. If so, it would take Joann several days to get over her embarrassment. Tuning in again to the pastor, Jim Henry thought he had missed very little. The homily was one that had been, and would be, repeated at thousands of funerals in thousands of southern churches.

The funeral service was short, of necessity. It would be dark soon after eight. Joann walked with the constable to the cemetery. Fewer people were there than had been at the church, for many were hurrying home to ready themselves for bed. While virtually everyone would be up by five thirty the next morning, many rose at five. As they walked, and when they stood around the open grave, Jim Henry continually scanned the group. Not all the Red Men had come to the burial, probably just the most loyal and active. But he saw Broadus again, and Rat Tail.

As the pastor spoke prior to the interment, Jim Henry's thoughts wandered again. The words used here were familiar, he thought, little changed from funeral to funeral. His next thought was, this is phony, just something for the pastor to recite. But then he thought no, perhaps these old, very old, words are instead comforting. They had been recited over his father, and would be over his mother. They were spoken over his grandparents, and—if a clergyman had been found on what was, in those distant days, the western frontier—they had been spoken over his great grandparents, and so on back in time.

Shovels of dirt thumped on the wooden coffin and Jim Henry

put his arm around Joann. "We'd best be gittin' home. It's near 'bout dark." As she leaned into him he thought how great it was just to be alive. Then, scanning the scene one last time, he saw Rat Tail was still there.

"Hmmm," the constable muttered.

"Hmmm what?" Joann asked.

"Oh, maybe nothin'. Maybe somethin'."

DAY TEN

As the couple sat eating breakfast, Jim Henry said, "I'm afraid today's the day. If I can't arrest somebody for killin' Snag, Forrest Hames is gonna git on the sheriff, and the sheriff's gonna git on me, and I'll wind up havin' to arrest ole Rafer. And I don't believe for one minute he done it."

"So you're going to forget about Mae Belle?"

"Well, in a way. Maybe not. I don't know. I'm still thinkin' Mae Belle's murder is tied in with Snag's. 'Course I don't know exactly how—I maybe know how Mae Belle and Snag are connected. But it's probably a stretch."

The constable buttered another biscuit.

"Ah, Lord help us! I gotta pull off a miracle—or git mighty lucky."

Joann chuckled, "How're you going to go about pulling off this miracle? You're not really all that good at praying."

"That's probably right. But I've got a more down to earth plan. I'm thinkin' I ought to spend some time along Railroad Street. Somebody just might have seen Rat Tail goin' up along the river to meet Snag."

"You still think it's Rat Tail? I thought that idea was pretty weak. You think he killed Mae Belle too?"

"No, I don't *think* I believe that. He might've, I guess. But, well, I ain't got that part figured out yet. We'll see."

* * *

Jim Henry sat on the steps of the bandstand. From there, he could see Rat Tail's house. He counted four other houses from which one could easily see anyone going to the river and along the river path, into the uninhabited stretch that ran from the park up to Corn Mill Creek. He sighed and muttered, "I guess I got four chances."

At the first house, the constable found three small children and their grandfather, Miles Hatchett, who came limping to the door.

"Mornin' Miles. How're things with you?"

"Well, I'd tell you if the young 'uns won't here. But I can't use that sorta language 'round them. Come on in."

"Arthritis actin' up, is it?"

"I reckon; that's what they say. But I believe that there's just a fancy name for 'done wore out.' My knees hurt, my shoulders hurt, and I can't hardly do nothin' with my hands."

"That's a shame. You worked up 'til about two year ago, didn't you?"

"Yeah. Up 'til then I could make a go of it, even if I was a-hurtin'. Now all I can do is set around. Well, ever once in a while I can walk down to the river and fish a little."

The old man looked around. A rocker sat by the front window. It was draped with a quilt. No doubt it was his favorite chair, and where he spent most of his days. He went to the chair, slowly sat and then made shooing motions with his hands.

"You young 'uns go on out front and play. But stay 'round where I can see you. Don't go around back. If you do, I know you'll be down toward that river!" Then to Jim Henry he said, "What can I do for you Jim Henry? I ain't got no whiskey in the house—my girl won't allow such."

The constable chuckled, "I didn't think you were bootlegging Miles. Not now anyway. But I'm still worryin' at who killed Snag a week ago Saturday."

"Ain't made no progress then?"

"I wouldn't say that. I know pretty well some who didn't do it, and I think I know, maybe, who did do it. But it's all just my reckonin'. I ain't got no proof; so I'm out lookin' for it."

"And I'm one that's gonna have it?"

"Miles, that just might be. Can you recollect seein' anybody goin' up that river path toward the creek the day Snag was killed?"

"Goodness Gracious, Jim Henry! I have trouble rememberin' if I've had my dinner."

"Well, just think about it. You got a pretty good position here to see folks comin' and goin' along the tracks and along the river. Who've you seen?"

The old man sat silently rocking for a time. Finally he began to answer.

"I reckon I seen ole Snag goin' up by the river more'n I seen anybody else. He was right regular. I wondered if he had some 'shine hid along the river bank somewhere."

There followed another lengthy silence.

"Saw colored folk goin' by the river. Not often though, and not nearly as much as by the tracks o'course. And, ... oh, lotsa folks one time or another."

Jim Henry was disappointed in Miles' report. He wondered how to proceed. Then he had a thought, and he chuckled.

"Well, I bet ole Rat Tail never goes up the river. I expect Eloise keeps him on too short a leash."

Miles grinned and slapped his knee. "She's a piece a work all right. I hardly ever see Rat Tail outta the house, 'cept to come and go from the store. But, now, I believe I did see him go up the river one time. I noticed it special 'cause I seen him out so seldom."

"When was that, Miles?"

"Oh, Lawdy! I don't recollect."

"Was it recent?"

"I just couldn't say. My memory's about like the rest of me, done wore out."

After a further half hour's conversation, it was clear nothing more could be learned from the old grandfather. The constable felt certain he was so near. And yet, he knew, he was still so far away. He took his leave and moved to the next of the four houses. There he found two very young children in the charge of a black teen age girl. Nothing could be learned there.

Jim Henry moved on to the next house with reluctance. This was the home of Mildred and Floyd Baxter and their mentally handicapped son, Roger. Jim Henry was always uncomfortable around Roger. He did not know how to interact with the boy. Moreover, while he felt tremendous sympathy for Roger and the entire family, he also felt guilty, guilty because at base he just wanted to avoid the handicapped child. Roger was seventeen, but mentally he was on a level near that of a, below average, three year old.

Taking a deep breath, Jim Henry mounted the porch and knocked at the door. Immediately he heard someone running and Roger appeared at the door. The boy looked silently at Jim Henry, bouncing up and down with his feet never completely leaving the floor. He then slowly reached out and put his hand on the constable's cheek. Mentally steeling himself, Jim Henry smiled and said, "Hello Roger." Then Mrs. Baxter came to the door.

"Roger, leave Constable Tate alone. Why don't you sit in the swing?"

"Hello Mildred, you got a minute to talk?"

"Of course I have, Jim Henry. Here, let's take these chairs on the porch."

The teen age boy began to swing slowly back and forth while making stylized hand gestures a few inches from his face. Suddenly he dropped his hands and said, "Dad whips me with a belt."

"Oh good heavens Roger, he does not. Jim Henry, you know how Roger makes up stories. His father has never taken a belt to him."

"I'm sure he hasn't, Mildred. I know Floyd's a good father."

"Sometimes he is a little harsh with Roger, but he's never done more than swat him on the bottom with his palm."

Mrs. Baxter looked uncomfortably at the floor, then at Roger, and finally at Jim Henry.

"But you didn't come here to talk about Floyd. What can I do for you Jim Henry?"

"I'm wonderin' if you can recall seein' anybody goin' up the river path toward the creek a week ago this past Saturday?"

"A week ago this past Saturday? Oh, oh my, that would be right about the day Zebulon was killed."

"Yes ma'am. It would be."

"Well, right off I don't think of anybody. But so many folks go up that way from time to time. I just don't know."

"Give yourself some time. Just think who you've seen goin' along up the river there."

As Mrs. Baxter sat thinking, Roger said, "Biscuits and gravy. Biscuits and gravy."

"Oh Roger! You had a big breakfast and it's not time to eat yet. Just you swing and let me and Mr. Tate chat for a while."

"Biscuits and gravy."

"Roger! Let's not talk about eating."

Roger began hitting his left forearm with two fingers of his right hand.

"Roger, please stop hitting yourself. You'll have a bruise on your arm."

Mrs. Baxter moved her chair nearer the swing and held Roger's hand. After a few moments she said, "I can remember seeing people goin' that way. But I'm not sure I can remember when I saw them. I stay busy most of the time. I don't often pay attention to comin's and goin's."

Once again Roger volunteered, "Dad whips me with a belt."

Mildred sighed, "I do wish Roger would stop that. You know how folks are. They'll believe most anything."

"Oh Mildred, I don't think folks—" Jim Henry sat staring at Roger.

After a moment Mildred asked, "What did you start to say Jim Henry?"

"Ummm. I don't recall. I lost my train of thought." He smiled, "But I thank you for your time. And I thank you Roger. I'll just say goodbye now."

Roger said, "Goodbye, goodbye, goodbye."

"Goodbye Roger."

Jim Henry walked down the railroad, headed for the company store. It's so simple, he thought. I'll just tell Rat Tail that someone saw him goin' up the river trail. I'll say they saw Snag a-goin' up that way too. Maybe that little lie'll shake him enough so he'll admit he's the one shot Snag.

As the constable was about to enter the store, he felt a hand on his shoulder. "Jim Henry. I hear you was lookin' for me yesterday."

Turning, he saw Rush Hamrick. "Oh, ummm, that's right Rush. Forrest Hames tells me there may be some dynamite left over from when the railroad track was bein' laid. He says you're the man to see about that—says if they is any it's in the train shed."

"Well I'm the man alright. But Mr. Hames is wrong. We did have some dynamite in there, but kids git in that shed of a day, especially if one of the cars is there, or the engine."

"So, they's not any?"

"Oh they's a half dozen sticks. I recollect that for sure. But Hames ought to know where it is, because we moved it to that little storage building behind his house."

"You reckon it's still.....you reckon...."

Jim Henry stood speechless for a time and the puzzled outside foreman just looked on. Finally, Jim Henry said, "Well I'll be a son of a gun."

"What are you goin' on about Jim Henry?"

Jim Henry just shook his head. "Rush, you think that dynamite's still in Hames out buildin'?"

"I expect. Is it important?"

"I think it is. Could we check? Jubal won't mind if it's the both of us lookin' in that shed."

* * *

The two men knocked at the door of the Hames house and Jubal immediately appeared.

"Jubal, you remember that we stored some dynamite in the shed out back here?"

"Yes sir, Mr. Rush, I remember that."

"Well, I need to check on it. I don't think Mr. Hames would mind."

"I don't know, Mr. Rush. Mr. Forrest's not here."

"We won't take nothin'; we just wanna take a quick look. I'll go directly and tell Mr. Hames we was in there."

Without waiting for an answer from the black retainer, the two men walked to the back of the house and into the storage shed. It took only a moment to locate the dynamite. There were five sticks.

"Rush, you sure they was six sticks?"

"I am. That dynamite's my responsibility. I was careful to count what we had left."

Jim Henry shook his head; his shoulders sagged, "Well, I'll just be damned. Colder than a witch's tit."

* * *

Jim Henry went to the livery stable for a buggy and then drove to his house. As he came in, Joann called, "Is that you Law Man?"

"It shore is, and I'm fixin' to act like a law man."

Jim Henry went to the chest in the bedroom and was removing his revolver when Joann entered.

"What? What's happening? Why's there a buggy out front?"

"I'm about to arrest somebody for murder. I'll have to drive 'em to jail."

Strapping on his weapon, Jim Henry headed back out the door.

"Who Jim Henry? Jim Henry, where *are* you going?"

"I'll tell you about it later."

"You be careful!"

* * *

At Jim Henry's knock, Eloise Summie appeared at the door.

"Why hello constable. We don't see you very often. Come in."

"I don't need to come in. I'm afraid this ain't no social call."

"Oh, come on in and I'll get you a glass of tea."

She walked away back into the house and Jim Henry, of necessity, followed.

"Here, take this chair."

Jim Henry sat. "Don't git no tea. Ain't neither one of us stayin' to drink tea. I'll set while you gather up things you might wanna take with you."

"Whatever do you mean? Maybe you should tell me why you're here. You seem awfully troubled."

"I'm troubled all right. I'm arrestin' you for murder, and takin' you to jail."

"Why land sakes! Who am I supposed to have murdered?"

"You know very well. You killed Mae Belle Hudson."

"Why would I kill Miss Hudson? And more importantly, how could I have managed to kill Miss Hudson?"

"I reckon you had your reason, and I'm pretty sure I know what it was. But I surely do know how. You went into Mae Belle's house Monday when you was deliverin' them flyers about the revival, and you hid a stick of dynamite in her stove."

"My, my, constable! Of course I went into her house—briefly. At any house where no one was home, I stepped inside to leave a flyer where it would not blow away."

"That's right. That's why nobody remarked that you had been in the Hudson house. It was the most natural thing in the world for folks to see you step in to deliver a flyer. But you delivered a lot more than a flyer at Mae Belle's."

"How can you think that? And since you do seem to think that, where in the world would I get dynamite?"

"I believe you got it just by chance. You was in that storage shed behind Forrest Hames' house on the night of his dinner. In that shed, you saw six sticks of dynamite. That must have been when you hatched the plot to kill Mae Belle. I checked just a while ago. They's only five sticks there now, cause you put one stick in yer hand bag. That's the stick you put in Mae Belle's stove."

Afterward Jim Henry would remember that all at once there seemed to come a chilling change. It was as if a façade had been torn away.

"Well, that's a pretty theory constable. But you'll never get a jury to believe it was me killed that hussy!"

Hatred boiled in her eyes, hatred suddenly replaced by fear. There was a deafening boom just at Jim Henry's right ear. As he fell to his left away from the sound he saw a bloody splotch expanding on Eloise Summie's chest. Jim Henry hit the floor grappling at his revolver. He was certain that in the next moment there would be another blast, and he too would be dead.

But no second blast came. Jim Henry rolled onto his back and saw Rat Tail standing, looking at the body of his wife. Slowly the shotgun slipped from his hand, and just as slowly Rat Tail sank to a sitting position on the floor.

Jim Henry got to his feet with his ears ringing from the blast and his cheek smarting from powder burn. With revolver in hand, he stepped over Rat Tail and picked up the shotgun. The constable's hands began to shake, then his knees followed suit. He moved back to the seat he had just fallen from, and fell heavily back into it.

The two men sat without speaking. Presently, Jim Henry became aware—more by vibrations in the floor of the house than by sound—of people on the front porch. In his mind's eye he saw people running to see what had happened. They were drawn to the sound of the shotgun blast, he thought, like iron filings drawn to a magnet.

The constable went to the door and called out, "This here's Jim Henry Tate. I want ever body to stay outta this house. They's nothin' can be done to help. Just stay out!"

As Jim Henry walked back into the room, Rat Tail looked up. Hoping his hearing had returned enough for him to hear the answer, Jim

Henry asked, "You the one that killed Snag?"

There was no reply.

"You was seen goin' up that river path. Snag was seen too."

Rat Tail first nodded, and then said, "Yeah. I shot that white trash son of a bitch."

When the ringing in his ears had somewhat subsided, Jim Henry went out onto the porch. There were about a dozen people, mostly those too old to work, gathered in the yard. It seemed they all asked the same question at the same time, "What happened?"

Jim Henry scanned the crowd.

"Would somebody go and fetch Amos Scruggs? Tell him we got another one for him."

One of the old men replied he would go after Amos.

* * *

Arriving back home, Jim Henry was famished. He had stopped at a country store on the way to the county seat and bought crackers and cheese for himself and Rat Tail. That had been woefully inadequate. Jim Henry wolfed down cold cornbread and buttermilk while Joann cut cold biscuits in half, buttered the halves and put them in the oven to toast. Then she began frying slices of livermush. When the biscuits and livermush were ready, she scrambled four eggs.

Joann settled herself at the table with her pad, pencil, and a glass of sweet tea.

"Now, Law Man. I want the whole story. You tell me later what I can write and what I can't."

Jim Henry grinned. "Well, first off, I was right. Rat Tail killed Snag. He just didn't do it exactly like I thought."

The constable stopped and ate several bites.

"So Rat Tail did kill Snag, and Eloise killed Mae Belle? What a pair!"

"Yeah, weren't they? Anyway, you sorta saw the key to the whole thing. You said—well you sorta said—Rat Tail and Mae Belle were lonely people."

Joann smiled, "And as I recall, you rephrased that and said they 'weren't gettin' any.'"

"Well I was wrong. They was gittin' it, from each other. Seems Mae Belle was some sort of distant kin to Eloise. Her and Rat Tail met at a family reunion one time. Like I said—or you said—they was both lonely, and one thing sorta led to another, I guess. Them things do happen."

There was a pause for more eating.

"Seems them two couldn't git enough of each other. Mae Belle's dad was a Red Man, so he was outta the house right regular. Rat Tail joined the Red Men so he'd have a reason to be away from Eloise, and of course he didn't go to meetin' all that often 'cause he slipped off to be with Mae Belle while Roscoe was away. I guess they'd of gone on like that, except Snag found out somehow. He started blackmailin' ole Rat Tail and Rat Tail started stealin' a dollar or so from the store ever so often."

"Is that why he killed Snag?"

"I guess you'd say yes—about the blackmailin'. Rat Tail said he was happy enough to give Snag some money, and would've kept doin' it, but Snag couldn't be satisfied with that. That Snag was a piece a work. He told Rat Tail that along with the money he wanted to 'share' Mae Belle too."

"He was about as low as a man can get."

"I reckon. Well, Rat Tail'd not go along with that, but Snag kept pressin' him. So finally Rat Tail told ole Snag that Mae Belle would meet him down by the river, where that path comes down from The Line. Only it was Rat Tail met him. He went down there with his shotgun and waited for Snag. There weren't no trees big enough for him to hide behind, but he saw a piece of oil cloth sort of up under some ferns and weeds and such. He laid down on that and slid back under the overhangin' brush. Snag showed up and stood lookin' around. Rat Tail called out to him. When Snag turned toward him, Rat Tail blasted Snag and that was that. So, you see, Rat Tail was on the ground when he shot Snag, just like I said."

"But Snag didn't knock him down like you said."

"A man can't always get ever little thing exactly right."

Joann laughed, "I know one that can't."

"That's not very generous, and after I give you credit for sorta findin' the solution. Without you I'd not have figured out Eloise killed Mae Belle. You saw her in that shed plunderin' around. When Rush told me about the dynamite in that shed, and when we saw a stick was missin', I knew Eloise had to be the one."

Joann looked doubtful. "But a jury might not have been convinced."

Jim Henry chewed for a moment, and then said, "That's right enough. But Rat Tail had come home a little early to eat, and he heard me tellin' Eloise what I knew. I guess *he* was convinced."

Jim Henry took a drink of milk

"He must've really loved Mae Belle."

Joann sat looking at her hands as Jim Henry finished his meal.

"So this whole thing happened because of Rat Tail's carrying on with Mae Belle. What gets into you men? What ever possessed Rat Tail?"

"Well, he told me the whole thing started 'cause he wanted, just once, to mount a woman who'd enjoy it. I reckon she did enjoy it, and there they went."

SEVERAL DAYS LATER

It was a beautiful day. Wispy clouds floated in a blue sky, lending brief shade from time to time. It was hot—that could not be denied—but a breeze kept the heat from being oppressive. The buggy had a brand new roof to shield the riders from sun, or the unlikely storm, and the sleek young filly stepped eagerly down the road.

Joann was looking forward to a couple of days in Lawndale visiting Jimmy, even if it did mean missing some of the revival. Jim Henry was looking forward to being out of town for a time and, he and Joann both knew, he was happy to miss part of the revival.

Jim Henry also felt great relief at having solved the first murders in Boiling Springs' short history. Of course, he fully realized one murder had required no solving, and another would, most likely, have gone unsolved without a confession—a confession he wasn't sure he'd done anything to bring about. All this, however, did not diminish his satisfaction.

As the couple's buggy rolled through Sunshine, Jim Henry saw Ruby Charles standing outside the café, leaning against the wall. He tipped his hat to her. She spat and yelled, "You can still go straight to hell Constable!"

Joann gasped, "Why, what a rude thing to say!"

"Yeah, she's still mad about me taking Joe to the hoosegow. And I guess I was pokin' at her a little by tippin' my hat."

"Nevertheless, she should have better manners."

"Yeah, I expect so. She makes her way in a rough crowd though; it ain't no wonder she's a bit rough herself."

They rode a little further without talking. Then Joann asked, "Do you think Gee and Haw will ever wind up in jail for cutting up and nearly killing R. D.?"

"I don't rightly know. I don't expect they're dumb enough to show up 'round here again."

"Well maybe, but they might come through on the sly. They've both lived here for, oh, must be six or eight years. This has got to be home to them."

"Still, I doubt they'll chance comin' around. I've got to think they're in South Carolina, or maybe Georgia, to stay."

"So, they'll get away with what they did to R. D.?"

"I'm afraid they might. But it's likely they'll wind up somewhere where they's some real bad 'uns. They'll act a fool there like they did around here, and somebody'll just kill 'em."

"That would be wrong. They don't deserve to die—even if they are mean and wild."

"No, I reckon not. But they's probably no way for 'em to change now. Them boys just took a wild turn a good while back."

There was another lengthy pause. Then Joann said, "I feel bad about reporting Rat Tail and Mae Belle were carrying on like they were."

"I know, but it's gonna come out at Rat Tail's trial anyhow. No way it coulda been hushed up, you know that."

"Still, I feel kind of bad about it."

"I know you do."

After a bit Joann asked, "Why were you so eager to stop by the spinning room and give a copy of the paper to Vernon Ladshaw?"

Jim Henry chuckled.

"Oh, I just wanted to be sure he read yer piece. I was afraid he might miss it."

Joann thought for a moment and said, "There's more to it than that. What are you not telling me Jim Henry?"

"Me? Keepin' things from you? I don't think so."

"I'll find out eventually. You know that, don't you?"

"Maybe so. You seem to find out lotsa things."

As the two rode along they reviewed the events of the past two weeks, then talked about how Jimmy might be getting along. About five miles out of town they spotted a black woman walking down the road. As they drew along side it appeared the young woman was trying to hide her face from them. They rode past. Then Joann turned, looked back, and called, "Jim Henry, stop!"

Jim Henry drew the horse up.

"What in the world are you yellin' about? You scared me half to death, and you scared the filly too."

"That woman we just passed is LuElla. What's she doin' out here? LuElla!"

LuElla stopped well behind the buggy.

"Miss Joann, Mr. Jim Henry. What you all want with me? I ain't done nothin' wrong."

"Well of course, nobody thinks you've done anything wrong. You're just out here miles from anywhere and we wonder what you're doing."

"I can't be where I wanna be? I'm just walkin' down the road."

"Of course you can be where you want. We're just worried for you. The constable told me you were crosswise with your father. Does that have something to do with your being here?"

"It do and it don't. Why can't you folks just drive on and leave me alone?"

"If that's what you want, we can do that. But can we take you somewhere? It's hot and dry out here. Where are you going?"

"I don't see it matter where I'm goin'. I'm just goin'."

Jim Henry snapped the reins and the horse began a slow trot.

"Jim Henry, stop this buggy!"

With a sigh, the constable drew the horse up a second time.

Joann called, "LuElla, get in this buggy right now. We'll take you at least part way wherever you're headed."

Reluctantly, LuElla walked to the buggy, threw her satchel onto it and sat behind the single seat with her legs dangling off the back.

The next mile passed in silence. Then Joann could stand it no longer.

"LuElla, are you just gonna jump off the buggy when we get where you're going? We're going to Lawndale. Are you going that far? Is that on your way?"

LuElla sat silent.

"LuElla, this is just foolish. We're not your enemies. Why won't you talk to us?"

"Don't nobody need to know where I'm going."

Again the three rode in silence. Then Jim Henry chuckled and said, "Well I'll be! You're leavin', ain't you? You told me you was gonna leave before yer daddy found yer money. Now you're doin' it anyway. Where you headed?"

"Don't nobody need to know."

"Well, how you gonna make it with no money?"

Confidently LuElla said, "I got six dollars and twenty cents. I just got paid and I ain't give that pay to daddy." She paused and with considerably less confidence said, "I got some cheese and some ham biscuits. I kin work. I kin make it."

Joann turned and looked at LuElla. "I bet you're going to Shelby to catch the train. You wouldn't be leaving just to go somewhere you can walk to."

LuElla made no reply.

* * *

Jim Henry pulled into the Shelby railway station. LuElla took her satchel, walked a few steps, then turned and said, "Mr. Jim Henry, Miss Joann, I'm obliged."

As the young woman walked away, Jim Henry saw a watering trough and directed the filly toward it.

"Better let this girl have a drink before we go on."

"I should think so. She's got extra work to do. We must be going eight or nine miles out of the way. I'm surprised you brought LuElla here. Why did you?"

Jim Henry stepped down and began to pump water into the trough so the horse could drink.

"Well, I guess because of all them who's been mixed up in this mess, LuElla looks like the only one with a chance to git what she was a-wantin'."

AUTHORS NOTE

While it is true that towns named "Boiling Springs" exist in both North Carolina and South Carolina, the mill village described in this novel does not exist. Likewise those persons inhabiting this non-existent town are creatures of my imagination.

I thank my wife, Elaine Byassee Bailey, for her indefatigable assistance. She edited this novel more than once, and it is better for her editing. The responsibility for any stylistic awkwardness, or (unintended) grammatical irregularity, that remains, is mine and mine alone.

ABOUT THE AUTHOR

Don Bailey is a retired university professor, having taught mathematics at colleges and universities in eastern North Carolina, east central Iowa and south Texas. He is the author of a textbook, a number of technical papers in mathematics, and a history of his home town.

Don grew up in a small North Carolina textile village located just a few miles north of the spot where the Battle of Cowpens was fought in the Revolutionary War. As a young boy he worked in the weave shop, and other departments, of the textile mill around which the village was built. That textile mill is now gone, as is the accompanying village.

The Linthead Murders is Don's first novel. He lives near Hendersonville, NC, almost in the shadow of Mount Pisgah, and not too far from Cold Mountain.

www.ingramcontent.com/pod-product-compliance
Lightning Source LLC
Chambersburg PA
CBHW061205170626
46809CB00003B/1251

* 9 7 8 0 6 9 2 3 4 4 8 3 5 *